“To my son, Joshua, whom I wish could grow up in a better tomorrow”

Prologue

We have organisations for the preservation of almost everything in life that we want but no organisation for the preservation of mankind. People seem to have decided that our collective will is too weak or flawed to rise to this occasion. They see the violence that has saturated human history and conclude that to practice violence is innate to our species. They find the perennial hope that peace can be brought to the earth once and for all a delusion of the well-meaning who have refused to face the "harsh realities" of international life – the realities of self-interest, fear, hatred, and aggression. They have concluded that these realities are eternal ones, and this conclusion defeats at the outset any hope of taking the actions necessary for survival. - Jonathan Schell, *The Fate of the Earth*

Humanity has always been in a dance between hope and despair. The evolution of human history paints the illusion of progress. At the turn of the 21st century, we boasted of increases in life expectancy, technological advancements, economic growth and a rise in literacy amongst many other achievements. Medical advancement has increased the lifespan of human being and more people have access to education. On the technological front, machines are getting smarter and systems are becoming more intelligent. The world's economic growth has also expanded tremendously and raised the overall wealth of the world.

At the turn of the century, we overcame the Y2K bug and witnessed the tremendous benefits of technology in the contemporary experience. Yet, at the same time, technology festers a host of other problems. With the advent of social media and user-generated content, falsehoods abound, demanding the discernment of individuals if they wanted to stay abreast of what is real. The uncomfortable truth is that beneath all the progress, undercurrents of conflicts and contradictions still persist. Are we really thriving?

⍰

Inequality plagues our society. As the world collectively gets richer, the rich-poor gap has only widened, attesting to the failure of the existing systems in creating an equitable society. Wealth is and has always been concentrated in the hands of a small circle—hoarded, kept, and passed down through generations. While the super-rich indulge in excesses and maintain their extravagant lifestyle, the destitute wrestle with their survival.

The bailout of banks during the 2008 Financial Crisis bear testament to the social injustice that underlie both the sector and society—after the bailout, the irresponsible acts that fuelled the financial crisis continued, without a shred of remorse or recognition of the consequences from the people who caused it. Hubris and greed are at the heart of any financial crises. Bankers, companies, and the society at large have conflicting interests: Bankers at the top management are seized with desires to maximise their own bonus payout at all costs; shareholders and the capital market only focus on higher profitability and returns; while the society at large is stuck with the impact and costs of fraudulent activities, environmental destruction—footing the bill for companies deemed too big to fail. Today, it is unclear how much financial institutions and regulators have drawn upon the lessons of history when they continue to make questionable loans and approve risky assets and investment. They come up with "new", innovative asset classes and investment vehicles that merely repackaged products that carry the same systemic risks to the economy—all in a bid to haul bigger bonuses.

Power remains grossly unequal in society. Corruption runs amok. Blatant incidences of corruption by dictators and even democratically elected officials in power lay bare the deep roots of inequality and the lack of transparency and accountability. In certain places, corruption is endemic, resulting in severe economic difficulties and hardship. In some of the biggest scandal of our decade, we see chapters close without any increase in transparency and accountability. Big corporations and the ones in power continue to conspire for their own personal gain. Meritocracy is illusory because the prevailing system is upheld by an architecture of power. Mobility prospects are impeded by systems that favour those with resources, and intersectionality creates differentials in available options for individuals. It would take a complete overhaul of the neo-liberal logic and ideological systems for meritocracy to truly work.

Globalisation ostensibly removed barriers and created new opportunities for decentralised power. It seeded networks of trade that allowed less developed societies to grow and prosper, redirected the flow of capital towards emerging markets, and facilitated a shift in world power. Yet, when and where interests are threatened, there will inevitably be pushbacks. We see how nationalism, motivated by fear and insecurity, led to inwardness and protectionism.

Globalisation also brought with it a system of resource exploitation and infringement of human rights that amplified injustices globally—the perpetuation of income inequality across nations. Simultaneously, the seductiveness of rapid growth precipitated the indiscriminate plundering of Earth's resources. We are now in a run up against the ominous climate crisis because of the unsustainable exploitation of natural resources to meet demands created by unregulated population growth. The utter disregard for the environment is unsurprising—energies are always channelled into what is lucrative and caring for the environment clearly does not fall under that category. The move towards a solution is sluggish at best, occasionally regressive. We are too narrowly fixated on self-interest and entrenched within systems of power to be able to address the issue more concertedly. We navigate through the world like it's a zero-sum game—me vs. you.

The present epoch is rife with unprecedented social fragmentation. Societies are becoming more plural—a plethora of ideas, beliefs, values, and systems—without necessarily becoming more united. Without love, empathy, the capacity to dialogue and the commitment to live amicably, pluralism has led to increased polarisation. Where are the spaces for people to develop resonance towards shared humanity? Social injustice has characterised humanity over the centuries—human rights violation, modern-day slavery and discrimination, racism, and the perpetuation of classes and caste systems. In parts of the world today, social stratification according to ancient practices continue to deny people fair access and opportunities based on nothing else but a predetermined social class or family background.

Wars and conflicts continue unabated to this day. Presently, governments are bankrupt and running up against an economy that is unsustainable, crippled by the inability to provide sufficient public goods. Capitalist corporations and individuals multiply their wealth at the expense of their own country. Awash with the deluge of problems in the world today, the same issues of yesteryear, it is no wonder the younger generation is belted with despair.

We have had thousands of years to advance ourselves. But how different are we now, compared to our forefathers? Are we truly upholding human rights or are we more concerned about our individual rights? Where are we heading as a society? What is the better life that we are striving for as a human race? Have we been too caught up with narrow-minded obsessions and conflicts to even dream of a grander evolution of mankind? How can we harness technology to transform our way of living in ways that would forward us? Do we choose to continue in an endless cycle of conquering and destroying each other or aspire towards a transcendent future together?

The author provides a glimpse to a possible future reality under Pragmatism: where nothing is cast in stone, except for the goal of love and care for fellow men, and to strive for the progress of mankind both in physical and mental states. All other conditions can and may have to be altered from time to time depending on the people, times, and situations. The psyche is one of adaptability and openness—never to be locked in by pre-conceived notions, theories, and ideas of what should or should not be done. Nothing is too far-fetched to be implemented—the only thing that matters is what works and what doesn't. Scientific data and facts are the logic drivers of change. Ultimately, the proposed model is fuelled by a process of hypothesising, changing, testing, observing, followed by the repetition of the entire cycle. The destination: the progress of mankind.

This book proposes a vision for a possible future, not a roadmap but an imagination. It is a provocation. A challenge. If the current gears of society are in shambles, it calls for openness to entertain alternative propositions and to flirt with other possibilities. It provokes you to ask new questions and to consider the force of reality behind the proposal. If you get riled up, ask yourself why you are reacting in a certain way. What values are you holding on to? What are you striving for? Abandon all your preconceived notions and understanding; focus on what works best.

JAMES FY2775K
The Student

****

The year is 2170.
The place is Earth.
After various struggles and iterations, Mankind have arrived at the era of the Pragmatic State—a system which places the progress of Mankind and the betterment of society as a whole at the utmost importance while trying to achieve this by the most pragmatic means. No politics. No agenda. No discrimination. No unfair treatment. Everything is strived for equality and improvement to the Human condition. Now is the time for real progress and to demonstrate what the human race can accomplish together.

****

Gentle and warm yellow light shaft of light peeked through the full panelled windows of James' room, creating glints across the pristine and reflective surfaces of his room. He could hear the sleepy grunts of his roommate Garett, ruffling and shuffling through his sleep on the other side of the room. Suhan and MJ, James' other flatmates, were probably not up yet. There he was, up before the alarm rang. 8:05 am. 25 mins before the time he planned to get up. He turned to see his roommate sprawled over his bed, half a leg dangling from his bed, consumed by slumber. How blissful, he thought. He, on the other hand, was wide awake and could not go back to sleep even though he wanted to. Frustrated, he manoeuvred himself out of bed, put on his metallic wristband and swipe to activate ECHO. "Draw the curtains," he commanded. The curtains on James' side of the room gathered, waking up. The morning light charged him. He stood up and walked towards the windows. Beyond, he glanced at the luscious greenery weaving through the sheen of the city's clean pathways, buildings, and infrastructures.

The city was immaculate. Ornate buildings with designs that complement each other rather than compete with one another dot the cityscape under the Dome, which was more than 10km in diameter. The buildings did not have striking colours, being decked in muted silver-blue panels, spotless white bannisters and reflective black windows, but they still stand out owing to their magnificent sizes and exquisite designs. Living spaces, like the one James was living in were capacious, thanks to the availability of multi-level structures both above and below ground which allowed human urban footprint to be concentrated and minimized.

Extraction and manufacturing industries were fully automated, freeing up not just manpower, but physical space as well. A few of these skyscrapers double up as waterfalls, guiding rainwater down its sides. The water snaked around the bodies of the buildings, allowing people to enjoy the breath-taking spectacle when free-flowing swirling liquid dances around the magnificent skyscrapers. Other buildings were no less impressive, encased in carefully selected blooming flora and temperature-sensitive walls that changed their colour based on surrounding heat and automated shifting panels that morph the exterior shapes of some buildings.

From his room, sounds on the streets were muffled despite the hubbub of human and traffic on the roads, as noise dampening discs in the walls and the windows of his room reduces chatter. This view of the city was a sight James had only recently started getting used to as he had recently moved to this part of the Dome to further his education. Everyone lived in hostels nestled within schools before tertiary education. Like everyone else, James only moved out after entering university. Interlocking his fingers, he stretched his arms out and bent towards his sides. Time to get ready for school.

Following his usual routine, James freshened up in the shared bathroom. Standing in front of the mirror, he stared at the man with blue eyes who ran the razor down his angular jawline. He rubbed some hair wax on his hands and ran his fingers through his dark tousled hair. His square face holds a sharp nose that, coupled with his olive brown skin, hints at his biracial African-European genealogy. He is lanky, slim and toned, a testament to the long-distance runs he does, a routine that he continues to maintain since his high school days as a cross country runner. He gave his shaver a few hard shakes to dislodge his coarse hair, then placed it back in the drawer. Scanning his face left and right in the spotless mirror, he decided that he looked ready. The bathroom was seamlessly connected to the walk-in wardrobe that he and Garett shared. Without giving it much thought, he picked the first set on his rack, which was lined with outfits that spoke of his fuss-free personality: solid colours with casual bottoms. It was more convenient that way—he didn't like to waste time picking clothes. Time is better spent on other things. James was utilitarian that way.

He grabbed his interface, a compact scroll-like device in the size of a pen, got out of his room, and looked for Javier in the kitchen.

"What would you like to have for breakfast?" Javier asked.

"The usual," he commanded.

Javier was a customisable humanoid robot with arms and torso, but with a head that lacks intricate facial features. Like humans, his head contained memory and processed stimuli in a matter of microseconds. However, instead of eyes, nose and mouth, its face holds no features but only a smooth metallic surface. It is human-sized in order to help complete tasks that men used do. Instead of legs, underneath Javier's long torso are 4 wheels that allowed him to glide around. Javier had been programmed to carry out all household tasks, such as doing the laundry, folding clothes, cooking meals, clearing the dining table, washing the dishes, fixing electronics, mopping the floor and many others. As he manoeuvred, the sound of his machinery droned on, almost imperceptible to human ears. His arms mirrored the functions of humans, except he had four of those. Like clockwork, the gears and machinery of the 4-handed robot kicked into action. Deftly, Javier retrieved bread and jam from the cupboard and fridge, while pressing a button that ejects a previously closed cupboard unit. Subsequently, Javier manoeuvred towards the coffee machine. The familiar wafts of coffee slowly took over the room. The same humdrum of the everyday; the same scent of the morning.

"Breakfast is ready, James," Javier chirped melodiously.

"Thank you."

Taking a seat on the high chairs near the dining area, he sipped his coffee as he munched on his peanut butter and jelly toast. He left his apartment spotting a navy polo tee, denim jeans, brown loafers. He made swift swipes on ECHO and commanded, "Go to school." That brought his hoverboard that was parked underground to greet him when he steps out of the lift at the ground floor.

He walked to the lift lobby, activating sensors that brought a platform up to the 34th floor. Automated transparent doors slid open, and he stepped onto the round platform inside. This wall-less and cable-less lift comprised a flat circular platform inside a glass tube. Controlled on/off pulses of electricity runs through the inner walls of the tube, creating a maglev system that brings the hovering platform up and down for the residents to commute. From the vantage point inside the transparent cylinder, James could see the bustling city. He let his eyes trace the impeccable design of the buildings and streets within the Dome he lived in—a white metallic jungle woven and strung together by pockets of purposefully designed greenery and water features. The lift decelerated seamlessly when it approached the ground floor. As the door slid open, his hoverboard was already waiting for him, timed perfectly to greet him after he indicated that he left his apartment. Hopping onto his hoverboard, he took a seat and it started moving.

James stayed in the Sombrero Dome of Andromeda City, which comprised two other domes, Sculptor and Canis Major. Every city had a central Tower in the city centre which takes command from Keb where the High Order was located and housed all the governing Services. It was behemoth, standing out even amongst the other skyscrapers. It coordinated with the governing bodies of other cities all over the world to standardise the implementation of policies.

Out on the streets, the weather was cool—temperate all year round. Ever since the advent of the "Reformation" that established the current Pragmatic State system, scientific advancements flourished exponentially, and scientists found a way to regulate the emissions of carbon dioxide and temperatures within Domes all year round.

It was a mere 5-min hover board journey to school. He liked his journeys to school, although he missed living on campus for the past 17 years of his life. Yet there were perks to living in designated housing outside the campus. Being nestled in the residential areas meant that he was able to whizz by the different facilities in the city and take in the entirety of the city on his commute to school. Travelling through the city, the raw, moist, and dewy scent of grass filled the air, and the symphony of birds twittering can be heard. Nature and the built environment were intentionally interwoven in the design of Domes. However, every district was also designed with unique characteristics, which depended on whether there were conservation areas and historical buildings that were preserved. James' morning commute wound through Larra district, the white, minimal, and clean district for shopping and marketing experience; the Danza entertainment district with its eclectic mix of quaint low-rise and conserved buildings; and finally, the civic district, Quintin.

For James, every commute to school was a revision of the three mottos of society. On all buildings, the three mottos governing society were etched. With weight and gravitas these words loomed:

For progress to all Mankind | For benefit of the State | For living a meaningful Life

****

> In the Pragmatic State, the progress of Mankind in knowledge and development of virtues and harmonious living is the first pillar of society. Secondly, the stability, enrichment, and development in the economic and physical aspects of the State as a whole, will ultimately benefit the individual as well. When the first two mottos are secured, it paves the way for everyone to actualise the third motto-a meaningful Life. A meaningful Life is that through gaining more experiences interacting with the human and natural surroundings around

us, there needs to be a continuous drive towards learning, enrichment, self-realisation, and maturity of the Self to a higher level of moral conduct and virtue that reinforces the first motto.

The welfare of the Self and the State are deeply intertwined and aligned. The belief is that when the collective interests of society are placed above everything else, and the greater good is pursued, individuals will benefit also from the progress of the society and find that they are able to actualise a truly meaningful Life. The three mottos ground society and form the foundation of a functional society where social order is maintained.

****

All of James' life, the mottos were emphasised, reiterated, and inscribed into his consciousness. He understood the rationale and logic of the mottos cognitively—it made sense in ensuring that the society functions smoothly. However, there was a part of him that was not fully convinced.

His commute was about to end, marked by the final landmark of his journey: syllabus design department. It was a colossal sixty-storey building, asymmetrical in design. From afar it looked like "cubes" and units stacked in whimsical ways, perhaps mirroring the importance of the syllabus planning department in staying dynamic. James always felt withdrawn looking at the syllabus department. Perhaps it was fuelled by a scepticism he always held towards what the building represented.

****

In the Pragmatic State, subject matter experts--the best scientists, artists, mathematicians, architects--gather to design the curriculum of children from kindergarten to tertiary education. The syllabus is continuously updated by experts who are professionals brought in every couple of years to refresh the content based on new knowledge and changes in society.

****

The practice of getting experts to update the syllabus ensured that what was taught never goes out of date, but it seemed like an awful amount of power granted to a small group of people who had utter control over the psyche of every child born in society. How would they know what was best? Would they always act "correctly"? Deep in the recesses of his mind, there was a gnawing curiosity about why things necessarily had to be the way it was. Were there more robust methods for syllabus design?

For James, that was a jarring flaw in the system that should be apparent to all. "You think too much! The system has served us well and is functioning perfectly," Rashid would always say in his clear and crisp voice. James wondered if he was the only one who saw the potential flaw of the system. He had no answers, but every morning as he passed by the building he would indulge in the inquiry. The inquiry intersected with his growing restlessness at school. The school was a place of merriment and safety. Perhaps too safe. Too familiar. Too comfortable. Too unchallenging. James was now in the first year of university, in Common year. Scoring well was a problem for James. Perhaps that was the problem.

Shaking off the thoughts as James approached the faculty of the arts, the hoverboard slowed to a walking pace while he stepped off at the central drop-off point of the atrium. After James got off, the hoverboard moved deftly towards a separate storage area in the basement level of the facility. He could see Rashid waving passionately from a distance as he walked towards the lift. Gaiety never runs dry with Rashid. James loved Rashid for how infectious his joy was.

"Had a good sleep?" Rashid asked.

"Somewhat? I woke up 25 mins before the time I had wanted to and couldn't fall back to sleep," he replied. "Shall we head up?"

Heading up to the 25th floor and entering the classroom, they were welcomed by wafts of clean and fresh air that flowed into the building. The tables were immaculately organised room with tables arranged in a semi-circle. The lecture theatre was sloped, each row higher than the one in front. There was a meticulousness to the way things were designed—seamlessly and impeccably. As James and Rashid moved to the back of the classroom, James caught a figure decked in clashing prints gesturing wildly.

"Over here! James! Rashid!" Tomoe chirped.

"Got it," James called back.

It was history class today which was taught by Professor Koji in person, rather than a virtual lecturer as in the case for the Sciences. Discursive subjects were designed as in-person lectures to facilitate conversations and dialogues. Professor Koji entered the room, his gravitas sliced through the bustle of the class and grounded everyone. With a gruff voice, he asserted "Class begins now. You know what to do." Intuitively, James took out his interface, slid open to reveal illuminated buttons that allowed inputs. James put on his visor and was able to see the virtual screen transmitted from his interface. Every student was given an interface when they began schooling and they got a hardware replacement every few years.

The first part of the lesson was on the Holocaust, which was the extermination of Jews in Europe under Hitler's rule of Germany from the 1930s to 40s. One of the most horrific terms used in the Nazi regime was "Lebensunwertes Leben" or "life unworthy of life" which referred to people whose lives were unimportant, or those that should be killed. It was used to refer to the "racially inferior" or "sexually deviant". From outset, Hitler expressed his disdain towards the Jewish population and murdered civilians en masse. The policy later developed into the "final solution," which aimed for the complete extermination of the Jews. While it began with government facilities, where proper food and health care was denied, it culminated into camps that were built with the intention to murder and dispose bodies. Jews were systematically tortured, experimented on and exterminated. They were rounded up meticulously, stripped of all their belongings and possessions, and packed inhumanely into extremely deplorable living conditions. An estimated total of 6 million Jews were murdered during Hitler's rule.

"The atrocities of the Holocaust are a stark reminder of discrimination, racism and power in a world that was imbalanced. It is incredibly dangerous when twisted ideas take root in society" Professor Koji proclaimed. "History has taught us that left alone to human nature and instincts, we can be capable of great atrocities. We need to have an iron cast moral baseline in our mind that we should never cross, regardless of the situation we find ourselves in," he continued, "which is why the Pragmatic State became the solution. It is a poignant reminder of the mistakes of the past. By ensuring that proper values are taught to all from young, we eliminate the possibility of rogue individuals perpetuating extremist ideologies. Pragmatism ensures a stability in society that safeguards every individual's liberty. History is immensely fundamental for every single one of us in society because it points us to the recurring errors in history. Without a past, we will never know who we are, where we came from and how to move into the future. This is why the leaders have made history a compulsory subject for all citizens, so that everyone can internalise the gravity of past errors to avoid repeating them," Professor Koji added.

"How does the State understand personal liberties?" James interrupted.

"Uniform education ensures that the right values are taught in schools. Discriminatory acts are illegal by law. By doing so, it ensures that every individual in society develops common values in an environment where everyone develops the competency to appreciate and embrace differences. Not only co-existing under these differences but flourishing because of it. The same applies to religion—censorship occurs in instances where religion encourages physical conflict based on group differences," Professor Koji responded. "Every individual has the right to his or her own preferences and wants. But such wants must never infringe on another person's liberties or cause collective harm in society. That is where the line should be drawn. Discrimination cannot be tolerated."

History and politics fascinated James. The past sits somewhere between the imagined and the known. While events were historical, it takes imagination to reconstruct the past. It allowed him to imagine a bygone era and wander. Juxtaposing the chaos of the past with the existing order of society piqued his curiosity. It explained many of the practices he saw. The mistakes of history were the very reason why the Pragmatic State, along with the three mottos, helped to stabilise society. What he wished, though, was for there to be more of such dialogues about the rationale and principles behind these decisions. Somewhere in the syllabus department, a group of people decided what he learnt, and he wished there was more transparency to the process.

Much as James was enamoured with history, it was not what everyone was inclined towards. Wayne had begun the class nodding off and was now slouched over his table in full surrender to his disinterest in history. He cannot be blamed.

****

> The education system was designed to ensure that everyone could start on the same footing in being raised by the State. Regardless of one's genetic profiling, one would have to be exposed to the same wide variety of subjects. Based on people's intellectual disposition in the formative years, as well as their interests and desires, the system would provide the opportunity for them to develop, grow and excel in ways that helped them arrive at their maximum potential, which in turn benefits the society.

****

"If there are no other questions, I have an assignment for you before the next class. We will be examining the economic history of the 1950s to the 2000s. Research on the wealth disparity trends from in that period," Professor Koji announced. "I would like you to look into why there was a disparity. Identify what the causes of the income inequality and consider how the Pragmatic State eliminates that inequality."

As soon as class ended, Natalie chirped with a twinkle in her eyes, "Japanese for lunch today?"

"You know I'll always be down for Japanese any time," said Rashid.

"Let's go! I'm famished," Tomoe responded.

Whispering to each of their ECHOs, Tomoe, Rashid, Natalie, and James indicated their next destination to Japan hub. Their hoverboards greeted them at the precise time the lift arrived at the ground floor. They stepped onto their hoverboards and zoomed off towards the food hub. Once James got onto his hoverboard, he commanded "Group call with Tomoe, Rashid and Natalie." Through ECHO, the group chatted using their earphones while they are travelling to the hub.

"Did you guys see Wayne nodding off during class just now?" Tomoe chuckled, "Classic move."

"I suppose history isn't for everyone," Rashid commented. "I pity him for needing to take history. But it is a necessity because it helps us learn our history, recognise our failures, and avoid repeating mistakes. Besides, getting exposed to subjects that we may not have been profiled to be good at or interested in the only way the system creates equal opportunities to develop interest in subjects without pre-determination."

"Yeah, I've been in class with him for biology and boy, is he attentive in that class." James chimed in.

There were different cuisines available at the hub on campus, cooked and dished out by robots. Students could order the food through their ECHO whenever they want, and the food would be prepared within minutes. Some of the newer students were strolling around looking at the different food stalls, unfamiliar with all that was offered. A cacophony of smells and sounds lingered in the air—the aroma of grilled meat, that iconic sweet scent of stir-fried caramelised onions, the sizzling of bubbling butter, the smacking of lips and grinding of teeth.

Serving these hungry students were three different types of robots that worked at the hub tirelessly 24/7: serving robots, cooking robots and cleaning robots. Like Javier, they respond to oral commands. However, unlike Javier, they were far from human likeness, coming in dimensions that best suited their function. The serving robot was a ruby-red rectangular block on wheels, designed to be the same height as the tables in the hub. Upon reaching the group that ordered the food, a sliding phalange will push the tray that was on top of the robot onto the table. On the other hand, cleaning robots had white bodies with four arms. One of the arms had a thong-like apparatus attached to its end for picking up utensils, bowls and trays; another arm had a broom to sweep litter into the bin attached to the robot's trunk; the third arm had a spray at the tip; and the last arm was a rectangular piece with cloth wrapped around it.

With the myriad of options to choose from, be it Asian, American, European or African food, the motley crew were spoilt for choice. After throwing some suggestions around, they eventually settled for an udon restaurant, Kizuma.

"So have you guys decided on what you will be majoring in?" Natalie asked.

"I'm certain that film making is what I am meant to do for life. I cannot imagine doing anything else," Tomoe chirped. "The chat I had with Howard helped me to see things more clearly. It consolidated my thinking on what I would want to pursue next."

"Yeah, talking to my Guider also really helped me narrow down my interest to life sciences. It did help that she was also a life sciences major," Natalie added.

"Well, I am going into chemical engineering. I didn't even need any convincing. I knew it from the time I laid hands on my first chemical set," Rashid said.

James tapped his fingers nervously on the table out of habit. "How... how are you guys so certain? We've been exposed to the various disciplines and domains since young. According to our genetic dispositions we might be given more exposure in certain disciplines, without compromising on the exposure to other disciplines. But everything seems like a possible future for me. Am I the only one who finds it difficult to know if I'm making the right decision and getting life right?" James responded. "I miss Genevieve so much," he continued, "She was the one who introduced me to jazz and whisky. I don't have much in common with my current Guider. The relationship feels a little more instructional. But Genevieve... she would always have the right advice for me. Perhaps if she was still my Guider, I would not be as lost in my search for housing now."

The group went silent, unsure of what to say. James registered their helplessness. Perhaps he shouldn't have blurted all that. The sound of chopsticks clinking overtook the conversation as everyone busied themselves with their meals in the attempt to avoid talking.

Breaking the awkward silence, Tomoe asked, "So how's the search for an apartment coming along anyway?"

"I've only really started to get used to communal housing and now I have to look for my own apartment. I've tried looking at the Yurra region of Sombrero. Exciting as it sounds to be able to live in your own apartment, don't you guys ever think about how lonely this itinerant life feels? Your Guiders leave you and you're on your own. Sometimes that feels unnerving. Don't you guys ever feel lonely?" James asked.

"Sometimes, for sure," said Natalie, "but that's also why we have social groups and co-curricular activities that are so important in grounding us in a community."

"In a way, that is how life is, isn't it? You enter the world alone and you leave the world alone. You can never take anything with you, which is why returning all assets to the State when we die makes perfect sense," Rashid added. "Compared to the few remaining nations who have yet to convert to our system of Pragmatism, ours is a State with a far fairer system and distribution of resources. Truly pragmatic."

"I suppose. The basic allowance we get from the State covers the cost for all our daily necessities—food, transport and even vacation. Basic housing is also provided by the State. So technically, if I wanted to, I could choose to cruise by in life without working that hard for anything and still live comfortably," said James.

"Ah, but that would be a waste of your brilliance James!" Rashid jumped in.

It was true. James was extremely brilliant and topped his cohort in advanced mathematics and theoretical physics. Lately, he began to feel like there was not enough challenge in school that could keep him occupied. *Where does anyone find their drive in this society? How does Rashid keep up with his zest and enthusiasm? Why does it seem like I'm the only one grappling with the lack of drive for life and school?* he thought.

"I don't know about that..." he said.

****

In the Pragmatic State, children are brought up by the State and parental family relations do not exist. From 0 to 4-years old, every child is taken care of and exposed to early education in the capital city, Keb. When children are younger, they are taken care of by robots who tend to their physical needs. As the emotional needs of the children increase, the ratio of Guiders allocated to look after them increases. Guiders are in professional positions different from teachers who are tasked with education. They form bonds with their assigned children and care for their emotional and psychological needs. From 5-years old, every child will be dispatched randomly to different cities to start their formal education and begin living in hostels on campus. A Guider might not be assigned to the same child but will minimally be with a child for at least a year. Aside from providing emotional support and advising children on problems that they encounter, some Guiders also develop strong personal mentor-mentee relationships.

****

All that talk during lunch made James' head spin. He arrived at his empty apartment. Garett was not home. He trudged to his room and crashed right into his bed. That day, he just wanted to sink into his bed and disappear. While everything seemed good on the outside, there was a nagging disquiet about his lack of drive in life.

At times like those, there was only one recourse—artificial high. He spoke to ECHO, "Javier, prepare chemistry equipment." Javier entered his room with a tray of tubes, flasks, and chemicals. He reached out for his whisky bottle, which he kept in his room, poured himself a glass while waiting for the equipment to be set up. He took a sip; it was a day for an extra punchy and smoky night cap. He let the drink roll over his tongue, taking in the rich woody notes and smoke that finished spicy with lingering sherry. *Ahh*. He loved whisky for how there was something for every mood he was in. It was not a solution, but it was a good companion, medicinal at times.

"Equipment ready," Javier resounded and left the room. James set his whisky down, got up, put on his lab googles and began cooking up a concoction. Flakes was a contraband item (a drug that causes hallucination and high), but there was a loophole. While it cannot be bought, it was really just science—find the right chemicals and you will never run out of the supplies—a small feat for a chemistry expert like James. James had a preparatory mix ready—he prepared them in bulk periodically. All he had to do was to add the finishing touches and wait for reaction to complete whenever he needed an escape.

Five minutes later, Flakes was ready. Using the syringe, he drew out the solution. With sharpness and precision, he slowly injected the mix into his arm. Within a minute, he would be in a state of high. Escape was near. He was ready to flush the dullness, loneliness, and fundamental frustration about not knowing what to do with his life. Sometimes the high brought him clarity, accentuating his thought processes. Other times, like today, the high took him to a space where he could retreat into nothingness. His consciousness began to swirl as he looked up to his celling with detachment. *When did he fall back on the bed?* If only everything could pass. For now, momentarily, it could go away. He shut his eyes as if losing sight could somehow keep his being within his body. Blackness. Stillness. Quiet. Zen, for now...

****

> Every citizen in the Pragmatic State is given one free housing unit. While it is possible to own more than one property (the second one onwards bought by own savings), the free housing given by the State cannot be sold off although citizens can choose to return it to the State if it is not in use. In addition, the State also provides free education, transportation, and medical care to all citizens. Every citizen

is also provided with a basic allowance that will allow for a comfortable life, as long as they fulfil the basic role of contributing to society in one form or another. The amount of allowance dispensed differs based on age and changes with time.

****

***

"It's a beautiful place in the Heidel district of the Dome," the agent from the State's housing department remarked. He was showing James the apartment through a virtual video call. "The space is mandated size of 3,000 square feet as per the minimum stipulated by the State. You can see that there's also a balcony here," the officer said as he took James on an immersive virtual walkthrough using his visor. "The apartment offers an exquisite view of the city and overlooks the Loraine River. There are plenty of amenities around and the Korean cultural hub is right around the corner..."

Gesturing with his hand, James followed the officer by moving along in the virtual world. Moving through a virtual internal view of the house, the images were projected real-time from a drone positioned in the house. It was 4pm and the apartment had a yellow glow from the afternoon sun, which gave that space a warmth that he could imagine as his home. The apartment had full length windows, allowing copious light to stream in. The space in the living room was generous. *There would be space to play Skate Pro if Rashid came over*, he thought. Entering the master bedroom, James was taken by how capacious it was. It came attached with a full-length walk-in wardrobe and a bathroom.

"As you can see, the master bedroom is designed with Zen aesthetics. Elevated platform for the bed and a simple ledge beside the window for sitting," said the agent.

"The concrete-coloured floor with off-white walls is a nice touch," James commented.

The apartment looks incredible. It had a main living and entertainment area, study room, an exercise room, guest room and a lovely open-concept kitchen. The celling was relatively high, which made the apartment feel extra-large. He liked what he saw. He could picture himself building new habits and a new life in that space.

"So, what do you think? Would you like to visit this place in-person?" the agent inquired.

"Yeah, that sounds good. I'd love to take a look at the unit," James replied.

***

The following day, James arranged to visit the apartment with the agent. The Heidel district was lovely—there was a quiet charm to it. He took the time to walk around the neighbourhood. Strolling along the wide streets, he noticed that the neighbourhood had a different air to it. Perhaps it was the type of shops that flanked the walkway. There were less chain stores, more independent storeowners and hand-made craftsmen, which was a rarity in those days. In particular, there was an independent bakery, which he made mental note to revisit should he return to the district again.

Arriving at the building where the apartment was, he sat on a bench at the lawn in front of it. He was 30 minutes early and that would give him time to people watch. He sat down, watching the willow trees in the lawn sway and dance. The wind refreshed him. An old couple was sitting on another bench diagonal to him, having sandwiches. People walked slower, unhurried. The pace was lovely, he thought. James let his eyes wandered, taking notice of the willow trees around him, enjoying the refreshing smell of what seem to be the mixed scents of peonies and lavender.

"May I take the seat here?" a petite lady with bright eyes asked, rousing James from his momentary respite.

"Oh sure! Feel free," James replied.

"I just visited a unit in this building. This is a charming neighbourhood, isn't it? And it overlooks the Loraine River—you can't go wrong with flowing water bodies!"

"Ah. I am about to visit an available unit in this building as well!"

"If it checks the boxes, you should get it. You're looking for your first house as well?"

"Yeah, I've been looking for an apartment since the beginning of the year. I'm in my first year in the university at the Raifer Campus. And yourself?" said James. "...I'm James, by the way. What's your name?"'

"No wonder I've never seen you around. I'm Aria, attending my third year at the Nok Campus, doing history. You must be wondering why I am only getting an apartment now. I'm a little late to the game of getting my apartment because I was enjoying the company of my roommate so much. We are in the same major... ah the nights we spent just talking about the past, analysing and deconstructing it! Such precious moments. It's amazing to be able to share something you love so deeply with someone else. I am lucky to have had a roommate who shares my passion," Aria's eyes twinkled with excitement as she talked about history.

She was beaming with enthusiasm and a refreshing zest for life. James found it infectious. *Where does she find this drive from?* James thought.

"So, how did you know that history was your passion?"

"When do you feel alive?" Aria answered with another question.

"Well, I suppose it is when you feel a sense of satisfaction doing what your heart desires?" James said as his voice grew soft from uncertainty.

"To me, it's when I am moving along in my own path and inching nearer to my purpose. Studying history makes me feel fulfilled—it's like every moment spent on it takes me closer to who I'm meant to be. Who I can become, the actualised self," Aria said looking straight at James, with a grounded conviction and stillness in her eyes.

He has never met anyone quite like her. She was clear-headed and grounded. Yet at the same time, charged with a lightness in her presence.

"The actualised self... how do you know what is the correct path to take?" asked James.

"You will need to be convinced about your place in society in order to understand that," Aria answered.

"About that... I have lingering questions about how the system functions. Sometimes, it feels a little paternalistic. The invisible people at the top, whom we hardly see, making decisions on the way society is organised. I understand the logic behind the system, but some things are not properly explained. Such as the arrangement where relationships with offspring is not allowed. In my opinion, it feels a bit lonely. Friends... well they can leave one day, and so can your spouse," said James.

"I can't answer everything you mentioned but there's somewhere I'd like to bring you," Aria says. "Let's meet again to chat and I'll take you to a place I know you will love! Call me and update me about the apartment too!"

Before running off, they bumped their ECHO wristbands with one another to exchange contact information. James' agent had arrived and as James turned his back and scurried towards the building and into the lift, there was a stirring within him. *What does happiness mean for me? What is purpose*? James mused. She was gone but her words stayed with him. *How is it that someone so average can find so much zest for life?* He saw the glint in her blue eyes, glowing and steady, all certainty and knowing. There was a buzz on ECHO: *Let's meet at the Jeph Complex near the Tower next Friday at 10 am if you're up for some answers. You just might find it. –Aria*

She was incisive, striking at the heart of all the questions he had, giving form and vocabulary to his thoughts. *But how was she so sure that she has the answers?* The lift platform arrived at the floor of his apartment. "Message Aria: Sign me up," James muttered to ECHO to send a reply.

***

The sun was relentless, casting harsh shadows through the Dome's lattice metallic structure, which was hemispherical and provided structural support holding up the Dome's transparent outer casing. For all the illuminating qualities of the sun and its majestic glow, it was at the same time overwhelming, and more all-knowing. As he basked in the sun, Aria was walking towards him, brown hair

catching the light from the sun. She smiled when she saw James. "Hello!"
James greeted her and said, "So where are you taking me?"

She continued walking and led the way, "Did you get the apartment eventually?" steering the conversation.

"Yes, I did. I could imagine living in it and building a life in there. Although... I'm not exactly sure about how the shape or form of my life and passion will fill the space," James muttered.

They entered the Tower. James has never stepped into the Tower. "Perhaps to see your future better you need to clear the shadow of doubt you have right now. Follow me," Aria said as she led him to the side of entrance. *Strange. In a restricted area like this, how could Aria enter the Tower?* Before he could process that thought, Aria gestured for him to follow.

Trailing behind Aria, James eyes looked up, taking in the perfect concentric circles of corridors that seem to stretch into the heavens above. His mood lifted; his slight anxiety placated a little by the pulsing gradient of pastel lights emitted by light screens that line the outer banisters of every floor. With each slow pulse, the colours change ever so slightly, morphing from cyan to thistle to chartreus, creating a visually calming domain for visitors. The Tower was the brain of the Dome, where the Core was—directing traffic, regulating temperature within, storing personal data about its citizens and footages from different places, dispatching supplies, and managing all regulations and policies among other things. Aria motioned for him to keep up. *Of all places, why would this brunette he just met beckon me to follow her here?*

A few Services personnel walked past them but paid no attention to the two of them. *If we are there, that means we have to be authorised.* No one seems to be paying attention to us. *Or maybe they are just too busy with attending to the whims of the Dome, making sure that the logistics satisfy the population's welfare... or maybe...* James' mind wandered, trying to comprehend what's going on as Aria and him took the lift to the 37th floor of the Tower. She flitted out of the lift excitedly and James trailed behind, piqued by her excitement. Arriving at the front of a grey door, the door slid open upon detecting her security pass, ECHO. Aria said, "This is the archives facility about the things in the past. There's restricted access, so only designated people get access to this facility. I've brought you here today in secret and I hope you'll find the answers here, just like how I found mine."

The archive room was an empty room with a slightly raised, circular platform in the middle of the room. Aria took a step onto the platform, which activated the system. A holographic interactive AI figure appeared in front of them.

"Good afternoon, my name is Gretchen. What would you like to find out today? We contain centuries of accumulated data," said the hologram.

Aria turned to James and said, "The AI is an interactive information request module of the archives system capable of consolidating and amalgamating information based on any queries you have." She continued, "You mentioned the emptiness that comes with the lack of attachment to anyone in this life, and a loneliness caused by the transience of relationships. Too little explanation or justification is given for the prevailing practices. Why don't you ask Gretchen about that?"

"Tell me why familial relationships are not allowed by law," said James.

The hologram disappeared and a video began playing. Beginning with images of social media, the AI pulled together a series of posts and videos of the excessive lifestyle flaunted by the rich—lavish cars, flashy pool parties and opulent displays of wealth. All that was interjected by news reports of the destitute in the suburban areas living hand-to-mouth and starving children in the developing countries. Gretchen then explained that wealth disparity was precipitated by the hoarding of resources by the minority of the super-rich, who then pass down the wealth to their offspring. As a result, everyone started on a different footing based on the access their parents' wealth afforded them. This structural unfairness was entrenched within the way society functioned before. Legacy and self-interests governed the way people behaved at the end of the day. Not many people were able to see the need to address systemic issues or to transcend beyond their own self-interests.

Familial relationships and the concept of legacy were found to be the primary reason for the degrading state of things in the past. As long as families and generations existed, there would always be class differences from birth. Meritocracy would always be a farce—some would always have a head start to access and the accumulation of wealth. The cycle continues and the insatiable hunger for wealth continually breeds greed and engender hoarding behaviour. It wedged a divide between people; the mentality of 'Us vs. Them' resulted in a lot of historical atrocities and imbalances.

It was appalling and obscene. His blood trembled at the blatant injustice and inequality that resulted from the hoarding of resources, wealth, and power. The wretchedness of human nature made him nauseous. But it made him think: if he had offspring or parents, would he end up acting in the same way. Would he be able to transcend his self-interests? In that moment, he was caught by his own question, arriving at the realisation that he, too, might defer to human nature if he ever found himself in that situation. The drastic measures had to be taken to combat something fundamental about humans. Then, it hit him. No system was perfect. In order to rectify the issue, eliminating familial relations might be the only way to stamp out hoarding behaviours—it was always a fight to safeguard humanity against their own instincts. The system acknowledged human nature in ways that were deeply humane. Without family legacies, the education system created a true starting point for everyone and genuine meritocracy. Arrested by the realisation, James asked, "Why...why were people never shown these things of the past? It convinced more quickly than any history class is able to."

"I suppose it's hard to tell if people would be able to take this information with enough astuteness. It is quite contentious after all," Aria said.

"Show me more," James asserted.

Gretchen brought up the original intent of the founders, who were the leaders of one major country in the early 21st century. At that point in time, they decided upon the principles of Pragmatism and initiated a long process of change. The successes of Pragmatism eventually encouraged other countries to adopt it. The principles applied to society was mirrored in the way education was designed, and the system where syllabuses were decided upon. There was a certain heavy-handedness required in order to standardise learning and to ensure that everyone was able to start on the same clean slate.

"I'm not sure about the high level of control that needs to be in place. It seems to suggest that humans are incapable of doing well on their own?" James retorted after watching the video. To that, Gretchen said, "Let me pull up details that demonstrate how such a control is necessary."

Gretchen cobbled materials and news reports of the deep flaws of democratic systems. People could never break out of the inherent instinct to grab power and protect their own self-interests over the society. Governments struggled with the ability to implement policies that truly benefitted the people because processes were always hampered by political infighting and lobbying. Ultimately, the rich and powerful continued to benefit and poor continued to be left behind until such time that the system hit a critical point of failure and reset itself.

"Left to their own devices, humans will always fall back on their selfish nature," Gretchen concluded. James was convinced, but a part of him wondered if that was too pessimistic a point of view of the human nature. Was there a middle ground where more people, after being inculcated with the right values, could take more ownership and have more say?

"I would like to believe that one day, we will develop the maturity and the acumen to act like mature individuals who are capable of acting in the interest of the collective good. There has to be a better way to organise ourselves to ensure a balance of control," James said.

"Not everyone is capable of coming up with policies and designing systems in society. It is really up to people who can see these issues to wield the courage to devise better mechanisms," Aria said while staring intently into James' eyes. "What you have been seeing is but a small fraction of the reality and considerations that exist."

James was aware of what Aria was implying. His heart thumped louder, and he felt his blood pulsating through his veins. He recognised that his assumptions and understanding of the system were only a slice of reality. Arrogance drove him to think that he had it all figured out and that his constant wallowing was justified. "All I was able to see before were the jarring flaws of the system, without consideration of the other realities that existed to inform the structures of the society."

As they left the building, Aria commented, "I think you've found some answers today. Keep asking them and pushing the boundaries. That's how we can hope to progress."

"There's so much to think about. I will need to take more time to chew the cud," James replied.

"Take your time," Aria wrinkled a smile. "Well, I have to go now. But please, work through what you got out of this visit. I know it was something."

"It definitely was. And I must talk to you again once I've figured this out."

"I suppose."

"I'll contact you, Aria."

"Sure!"

Aria graced across the atrium of the complex with utmost glee, hopped onto her hoverboard and steered off. James got onto his hoverboard and watched Aria turn into a corner. Once out of sight, Aria began to glitch. By the time she arrived at the end of the quiet street, she disappeared completely, leaving the hoverboard on its own, floating by.

While he may not have all the answers now, James was rejuvenated by the visit to the archives. He might not know exactly how his life will pan out, but he had a more definite goal and drive. Surely, there must be something he can do to put his intelligence to better use. Drugs had been but an escape from the reality of things. Bit by bit, he was starting to understand that empathy could exist within a system with hard rules. Aria was right. Improvements to the system must come from the people who are able to see through the flaws and rise up to the challenge of re-designing systems and policy. That might be where he might start moving himself towards.

James got back to his apartment. Tired but energised inside. He sat down on the couch in the common space, resting but breathing with a new-found conviction. “Message Aria—Today has been immensely pivotal for me. Thank you,” James commanded ECHO. “Error 607. User not found,” ECHO replied.

Dave 2H44289 and Kai Ling E40830L

The Couple

"Is spacecraft 80E ready for launch to Mars?" Dave asked through the mic in the command office.

"All's good on our end," said the voice on the other end.

"Good to go then," Dave broadcasted.

"Prepare to launch," the operator commanded. "In 3, 2, 1."

The sound waves and gusts of wind from the take-off spread across Moon Base 45X as the spacecraft took off. Spacecraft 80E was the second batch of civilian spacecraft to be sent to Mars after the first wave of the settlers successfully established themselves there 3 months ago. Dave watched the spacecraft take off on the screen from his command office, heart pounding with excitement. Moon Base was a steely oblong-shaped building that imposed itself on a terraformed clearing south of the Moon Station.

Dave was a scientist in charge of space flight propulsion and developing new technologies for space exploration. It had been years of work to get the operations of Moon Base going. Moon had been fully terraformed to Earth's atmosphere. After a decade of hard work, the Space Exploration Agency (S.E.A.) finally completed the multi-stage process of pumping air into the atmosphere, generating nutrient elements on the topsoil layer, creating water bodies, and seeding the Moon with various forms of vegetation. With the Moon acting as an interchange, people could get to deep space.

Dave was incredibly devoted and committed to his work, which he was deeply passionate about. He leaned back on his chair, interlocked his fingers and stretched his arms gleefully. He was done for the day. Being key personnel in the S.E.A., Dave was stationed on the Moon most of the time, returning home only once a month.

Space was the next frontier for humans. Having attained a level of technology on Earth, space represented the unknown and the never-ending exploration—a challenge that symbolised the constant drive for advancement and progress as a society. Since Mars was also fully terraformed, Dave's challenge was in trying to come up with a propulsion system to intergalactic travel and exploration feasible considering that the nearest Star, Proxima Centauri and the nearest Galaxy, Andromeda Galaxy is a staggering 2.5million light years away.

"Heading back to Earth today?" Howard, his colleague in space command asked as Dave got up to pack his belongings.

"Yeah. I'll be back at the Earth's HQ overseeing other experiments and tests of Project J2M related to the new propulsion drive required for intergalactic travel," Dave replied.

"Shouldn't you be taking breaks while you're back?" Howard asked.

"Some things just can't wait. And I just got news from the team on Earth that we might be on to something. Up till now, our propulsion drive was able to establish a stable wormhole linking 2 points far apart in space, to send over and receive sub-atomic particles and electromagnetic radiations, but unable to achieve structural integrity for physical objects such as a shuttle probe. I'm itching to get back to see how we can move things forward," Dave mumbled, half-absorbed in his own thoughts. "If we are not able to achieve a breakthrough, the project might get passed on to another team. We're close to arriving at a solution after all this time we have devoted to the project. Besides, passing it on to the next team at this juncture would simply be too messy. We have to come up with an alternate solution to keep the project."

"I suppose you could see that as the State's way of ensuring innovation and constant breakthrough by lending fresh perspectives when the research hits a block. Don't push yourself too much, Dave. But anyway, I've got to bolt. I'm needed at the Propulsion Lab looking into the inconsistent thrust issues that we're seeing on the newly commissioned Gen-4 drives. Try to get some rest, my friend!" Howard muttered as he left the command office.

"See you soon, Howard," said Dave.

He knew he was stubborn and overly protective about his projects, bordering on being competitive. He did not like that people got to reap what he had sowed, and he relished in the satisfaction of problem solving, seeing a project from start-to-end. Somehow, he had the impression that projects being reallocated was a sign of failure for a research team leader and equivalent to letting the hard work of the team go to waste. He was walking out of the building when he remembered that Alex was also at Moon Base. He had not seen him for weeks now due to their schedules. Spontaneously, he made a detour and headed for the Energy Generation Department. As he approached the department, a teeming mass of students greeted him. They were crowding in the gallery area of the department's lab and plant. *Ah, school excursion day,* Dave thought.

"Now, a Mobius Battery is a small device which can store huge amounts of energy by creating an inter-universe wormhole across an infinite number of parallel universes. Look closely at the bright orange unit 10cm in height, placed in the middle of the room," Alex said as he pointed to the bright device in the centre of the room. He was explaining to a group of 12-year-old school children who were at Moon Base as part of the school's curriculum and excursion. The staff took turns to lead the site-visits, which happened weekly. "Fundamentally, it deposits a small amount of energy in each parallel universe in the form of a Mobius strip loop and can draw down or deposit energy without any loss when required. With just one Mobius Battery, we can power a city for a couple of years!" Alex hated having to fulfil these duties. It was meaningful work trying to bring children closer to the operations of space exploration but in practice, it felt a lot like babysitting.

"Now, stay within the group without wandering about!" he bellowed at two rambunctious boys running amok at the back of the group. At that moment, he spotted Dave at the corner of the room, leaning against the wall, arms crossed. With a smirk plastered across his face, Dave sniggered at the "nanny duties" Alex had to fulfil as part of his job at Moon Base. He nodded at Dave, eyes rolling in recognition of Dave's mocking smile. With the help of his assistant, they herded the group towards the next stop. "Does anyone know what a Black Hole is?" Alex continued.

Bright-eyed, eager children raised their hands in a frantic and zestful manner hoping that they might get chosen to answer the question. He picked the blonde-haired boy with dark skin.

"It is something that sucks everything in!" he answered.

"That's partially correct," he assured. "When a star, which is a massive ball of burning gas, ends its burning cycle, a supernova occurs, collapsing and releasing a lot of energy in the process." The children continued listening, enthralled by the fascinating information. "When that happens, the star is reduced to a singularity—an insane compaction of mass. The resultant gravitational field is so powerful that anything that passes near a black hole's limit, known as the event horizon, would be sucked into it–even light!" Alex emphasized.

He gestured for the children to follow him to the next room where the B.H.E.G was explained further. The children trotted along, fully engaged by the novelty of the facility. Dave trailed behind, interested to catch his friend in action. Stopping in front of a hologram, Alex explained, "Scientists have learnt that when matter passes through the event horizon, it rips all matter apart and releases energy in the process. The resultant radiation emitting out of the black hole comes from the matter's rest energy. The Black Hole Energy Generator taps into the massive gravity pull of existing black holes by means of an Einstein-Rosen bridge, a.k.a wormhole and breaks down the mass of any introduced matter to release astronomical amount of energy in a short burst. In essence, we are "sacrificing" matter into the black hole to produce energy. With just a few kilograms of matter, we can fully charge up a Mobius Battery. This is how we create limitless, clean energy to power everything in the world and beyond."

Some children were wowed by the information, others were confused, and a minority was simply disinterested. As they wrapped up the tour, Alex and his tour assistant handed the children back to the charge of the two Guiders who accompanied the students to Moon Base. Slowly, they made their way out.

"What a sight to behold," Dave teased when Alex was alone.

Unperturbed by Dave's teasing Alex attempted to change the subject, "How was the second settlement batch to Mars? Shouldn't you be on your way home now?"

"It was smooth. Everything went as planned! I'm on my way home but I had a sudden thought to catch you before I go. I read from the weekly internal updates that Project B.H.E.G is making tremendous breakthroughs. I was curious about that and wanted to hear it from the horse's mouth."

"You workaholic! Knock off already," Alex said. "Well, since we've established 2 BHEG operating in space at about 500,000km from Moon, the challenge is looking at the miniaturization of BHEG to allow it to be safely mounted into a space station and to make it more stable in energy output and safety. We're looking into ways to scale down the BHEG size and constantly making improvements to the safety of the equipment. We're also testing the use of higher atomic mass particles instead of Hydrogen in order to create higher energy bursts to power the new Particle Cannon that Military Services is developing. And we might just be on to something!"

Dave was captivated—as he always was when it came to science and technology. These conversations always got him pulsating with excitement. He could go on forever. There was a creativity and craft in this pursuit that he felt was seldom emphasised, one that maybe no one understood or appreciated.

"Ahh, that sounds incredible! Keep me posted about the experiments. Who knows, perhaps a good idea might come out from your developments that could potentially tip the scales in the stalemate of my current research," said Dave.

"For sure, Dave! Perhaps the next time you're back on Moon Base? Let's arrange a chat! I could use fresh perspectives as well," Alex replied.

As Dave left the building, he stepped onto his hoverboard and headed for the Interstellar Express. Moon served as an interchange mainly for deep space travel and related fields of research. While there wasn't a large settlement here, Moon Base was made up of 3 Domes, identical to those on Earth. Apartment buildings were lined orderly, grid-like, intentional. The ivory pavements were meticulously designed and fitted with shops offering amenities. One would forget that it was Moon if not for the absence of animals and wildlife. Dave breezed through the town, eventually arriving at the Interstellar Express. He made a quick command to purchase his ticket via ECHO enroute to the station. "One-way ticket from Moon Station to Triangulum Station on Earth, please," Dave said.

His hoverboard lumbered to a stop as he approached the drive-through the gantry.

"Please scan your wristband here," the automated machine responded as a scanning interface extended from the machine. He did as he was instructed.

"Check-in successful. Please proceed to platform 43."

He proceeded and boarded the spacecraft. He picked the window seat—he liked seeing the outer space from afar—perhaps it was the ability to see outer space diminish in size that gave him the perception of being in control although there remained mysteries to be solved. A strange duality of beholding and yet not knowing. Dave looked out of the window and saw himself through the reflection—asphalt hair, sapphire eyes, tan skin—mind filled with anxieties about the projects he has. Through his frown, worry framed his countenance. The drone of the engines operating on electromagnetic pulses let off a low humming sound that mirrored the constant preoccupation that pulsated through him.

***

Back at home, Kai Ling was seated on the couch, legs tucked to the side. Her ginger-coloured short hair complemented fair skin but was contrasted by her jet-black irises. She was reading when Dave returned.

"Hey love, you're back" Kai Ling said tenderly, eyes brightened. She was perched on the couch in the living room and reading when Dave opened the door to the apartment. "How was the launch to Mars?" she said.

"It was good. Smooth. There weren't many issues that we had to resolve prior to launch. How are you?" Dave replied while giving Kai Ling a tender hug.

"Oh, just the same. Doing some reading on discrimination in society for the think tank discussion tomorrow," Kai Ling said gazing up at Dave. "Hungry? I haven't had dinner. We can get Javier to fix something up."

"Sounds lovely. How about Indian cuisine tonight? I'm craving for spice and curry," Dave said.

"Yea sure. Anything you want," Kai Ling said. Lifting her right hand where ECHO was wrapped around, she spoke, "Prepare Indian cuisine for dinner tonight. Preference for curry and spice. Leave the setting of the table to me."

Their home was impeccable and spotless. As a couple, they subscribed to minimal living. As much as they are able, they wanted their space to be capacious and breathable. Apart from art, their possessions were minimal. Intricate ceramics lined the recessed display along the walls of the living room. The couple, particularly Kai Ling, enjoyed the craft and spirit behind ceramics. The art of making ceramics was the embodiment of craft and functionality. Though a historian, Kai Ling is well-versed in philosophy and the arts. Culture, she believed, governed the soul of an individual. The bedroom and study room were peppered with traces of Kai Ling. Dave's touches in the house was seen in the living room, perhaps a parallel to the presence he has at home. Being away from home most of the time, his absence was also reflected in his possessions, or lack thereof, in the house. The research room in the house, however, was all his. It was a quasi-lab space with a whole gamut of scientific equipment for times he wanted to conduct particular experiments.

"Dinner is ready in five minutes," Javier announced to Kai Ling. "Ready for table setting," Kai Ling responded.

Getting up from the couch, Kai Ling walked to the island table where the kitchen was. She could leave it to Javier to set the table, but today, she wanted to make the effort. It had been three weeks since Dave was home. There was something in labour and effort that was irreplaceable. Conscientiously, Kai Ling set the table mats and the utensils, while taking in the fragrance and exotic mix of spice that wafted from the kitchen where Javier was completing the meal. Manoeuvring to the dining table while bringing the final dish, Javier announced, "All the food has been served."

Kai Ling did a quick check to make sure that everything was in place. After getting everything set up, Kai Ling called out, "Dinner is ready!" Minutes later, Dave slowly hobbled out of his room, still half-groggy from having fallen asleep. The aroma of Indian spices perked him up instantly.

"What a spread!" he exclaimed, energised by the spice and herbs.

"Tuck in," Kai Ling said gently brimming with satisfaction with her husband's excitement.

Dave rambled on about the research he is currently doing and the breakthroughs that were happening with Alex's project with the B.H.E.G. Kai Ling nodded to what he was saying without registering anything. She was waiting for an opportune moment to interject and bring up the research she did on childbearing. It had been a point of tension between them—the last time it was brought up, it did not end well. She had wanted to get to it earlier, but it didn't seem appropriate to bring it up while he was away on Moon Base.

"—and we would be making tremendous progress in terms of our exploration to Mars!" Dave said passionately as he reached for the garlic *naan*, dipped it in the butter chicken stew and continued with his meal. She was clueless about what Dave was prattling on about, but the momentary pause was her moment.

"So... I've been doing some research about giving birth and its effects on the mother. And about the care our child will be given," Kai Ling said after mustering courage. She realised perhaps she should avoid using the word 'our' for fear that she would start having attachments to her child. She made a mental note about that and continued, "I'm... scared, Dave. I'm worried about the emotional attachment I would develop after carrying the child for nine months... I'm afraid of the emotional attachment and the kind of care that the child would receive."

Dave stopped chewing, pursed his lips, and went silent. *Back at it again. Why are we going through this again?* he thought.

"Haven't we been through this a few times?" Dave said. "Why is it coming up again when we've already decided to go through with it? See it this way, it is our role as citizens to have offspring. I'm not sure I can fully understand your concern regarding care that will be given and the attachment you might develop. I believe the State has made preparations to ensure that child bearers are well taken care of. Besides, we've been brought up by the State too, isn't it? And we've all turned out just fine."

"I'm not saying that I won't go through with it but that I need a little more assurance and information. It's immensely daunting and without you around most of the time, I know it will be on me," Kai Ling asserted, raising her voice slightly. "Will you at least accompany me to the Infants Department to understand how this works? That would really help me."

Dave was too exhausted to argue. He could not understand his wife's perspective and hesitation. His heart was always set on the progress of mankind, through his scientific research and contribution to space technology. Everything mattered less, and Kai Ling knew it—he was never one to be overly attached. The emotional labour and conversation with Kai Ling were something that frustrated him as much as it upset her.

They continued with their meal. Silence wedged between them. The act of eating became the means to dissipate tension; chewing and swallowing bought time to digest what was happening. They went on to complete their meal in silence, but as Dave got up and left, he stated matter-of-factly, "Let me know when that visit to the Infants Department is, I'll be there."

***

"... How do we decide if an act is discriminatory?" Kai Ling asked. "I think the key is to define 'discrimination'. Everyone is entitled to believe that they have certain rights to act and believe as they wish. If the ethical framework for everyone is so different, how can we create a law that can determine if something is ethical?"

"Perhaps it is when harm is done and exacted on another person," Rohan said.

"But even then, it is difficult to determine when 'harm' is done. The sphere of morality is extremely nebulous," Kai Ling replied.

"At the moment, the law is built upon particular ethical principles and morality that will need to have the flexibility to admit the different perspectives. Yet it needs to be able to determine the discriminatory practices that damage the social fabric in accordance with the moral principles of the Pragmatic State," Peterson, a practising lawyer responded.

"It's been almost one and a half hour of discussion on social policy and discrimination," said Felicia, from the Welfare department and the convenor of the think tank group. "Let's take a fifteen minutes break and return to look at some social policies and examine how we can do this better."

The think tank group for Social Policy and Ethics met monthly to discuss issues pertaining to policy making and ethics. There were over 30 of these groups in the Welfare department that met monthly, each with a different focus and comprising experts from different fields. Being an expert historian and well-versed in ethics in philosophy, Kai Ling was courted to provide her opinions on social policy and law making.

"How's the book that you're writing coming along, Kai Ling?" Marianne asked.

"It's moving along slowly but surely, I guess. The research on social relations in the past is extremely intriguing because of the insights it reveals about the impact of economic models on the way people understood their relationship with one another and their duty to the society at large," Kai Ling said. "It's illuminating of how we can be organising our society better in today's context. But it has been absolutely painful because it has taken time away from the other work that I need to do."

"Are there any new projects that you are currently involved in?" Lionel interjected.

"Apart from lecturing in the university, I've been working with Ascend Industries recently to design an AI-based exhibition and education centre on the history of civilized communities that were organised on the principle of communal living. The objective is to reiterate the importance of community-centred approaches towards the organisation of society. But enough about me, how about you guys? What are the projects you are currently working?" Kai Ling said.

"Because of my background in law, I've recently been pulled into a sub-committee of S.E.A. to look into the law-making for the new colonies and space missions. We're delving into the legalities of space exploration and the laws that govern the new colonies," Lionel responded. "It's all pretty exciting to me. There are considerations about the parameters and the boundaries of how far development and intervention can go in our interaction within these new spaces. For example, what happens if and when we discover lifeforms on planets which we previously thought were not possible? What will be the principle of engagement and interaction?" Lionel explained.

"What a bold move to venture into laws in space and technology!" Marianne commented.

"Definitely not my forte, but perhaps they are interested in getting a diverse mix in the committee," Lionel said. "But apart from that, I am continuing with the work for Kirkland and Spriggs that I have been with, as and when the firm requires my assistance and expertise... And you? Marianne? I heard you've been roped into the Education Policy think tank group to work on refining the policies surrounding education. How has that been?"

"Yeah, we're constantly relooking at the processes involved in the upbringing of the child and how we can provide a better learning and growing environment that will ensure that every child will thrive in ways that best suit their capabilities and interests," said Marianne.

Kai Ling was gripped by the mentioned of children. "What are some aspects that the group thinks require improvements on now?" she asked, guilty that it was a personal curiosity in the guise of an intellectual question.

"Well, we are looking into deepening our analysis of the role of Guiders at different stages of a child's growth and how we can improve the programme for the Guiders, such that the care that is offered to children will be of the highest standards," Marianne explained.

Kai Ling replied, “Were there any discussions about the principles behind how Guiders are prepared and trained for the role? And—”

“Shall we gather back now, everyone?” Felicia voice interjected Kai Ling’s question before she could finish.

“Well, perhaps another time, Kai Ling. If there’s a chance, I’ll be happy to answer your questions” Marianne said as she gestured for them to head towards the seats.

Kai Ling could not help feeling engulfed in disappointment. She wanted to know more. To find clarity about the system of care.

****

Kai Ling’s work belongs to the branch of the Social Sciences and the humanities. In the Pragmatic State, there are key areas of development. These aspects were important in the Pragmatic State to ensure that the society continues moving forward so that citizens can be in better health and enjoy a clean and sustainable environment. The strong emphasis on sciences ensures that they will continue to have the energy to achieve that.

In terms of medical science, there is ongoing research on nanobots that provides non-invasive cellular repair against cancer, various types of organic and inorganic medicine, advanced virus, and DNA manipulation (slowdown of telomeres shortening in human DNA) resulting in a longer lifespan and higher quality of life up till old age.

As for environmental science, terraforming technology, which allows the manipulation and creation of different elements by atomic splitting of heavier particles, has been underway—for example, creating vast amount of oxygen by splitting Silicon, which is a very common and abundant element in the universe into Oxygen and Carbon, both of which are fundamental in the creation and support of life forms as people know it. Aside from that, there is also copious research on flora and fauna preservation, rejuvenation of Earth, and seeding life on terraformed planets.

In the realm of the physical sciences, Physics and Chemistry are equally important. In particular, research in Quantum physics in relation to space travel and elemental manipulations is also a key focus. Material Science is another focus area. Research is moving into the fabrication of super strong, durable, and light materials used in construction, space travel vehicles, fabric for clothing and materials of daily living.

Energy Production, Storage and Transfer (BHEG and Mobius Battery) is the technology undergirding the efficiency of production in the society. With the creation of unlimited clean energy, there is no pollution from the creation and transfer of energy. Generation of energy from burning fossil fuels and other raw materials have also been eliminated. The cost of economic production was also drastically reduced, giving a huge boost to economy and productivity. A lot of other related fields such as space travel and terraforming that requires gargantuan amount of energy becomes a reality. Across the whole of society, there is increased automation and use of robotics to replace manual labour.

The humanities, such as philosophy and history, are also important in anchoring the values of a harmonious society. Continued research and deep studies have produced great thinkers who are roped into schools, think tank groups and syllabus design. In terms of the social sciences, sociology, economics, geography, and psychology are important pillars of study that continually shape the design of social policies, interrogate social relations in society, and keep the policies in check.

****

***

“God, it’s been so long Kai Ling!” Alice exclaimed the moment Kai Ling opened the door. Without warning, Alice hurled herself at Kai Ling and embraced her in tight squeeze.

Chuckling and overwhelmed by Alice’s usual display of affection, Kai Ling said, “I’ve missed you too, my dear. This has been long overdue.” She loved Alice’s openness and readiness to express her love. Alice was always exuberant and ready to share rays of her energy.

“We’re so glad you both can make it today,” Dave said as he gave Joey, Alice’s husband, a pat on the shoulders.

“We’ve been looking forward to this gathering all week!” Joey said as he returned the pat with a quick hug.

“Come on in!” Dave said. “We’ve prepared steak for lunch today! Cooked and prepared by yours truly.”

Joey and Alice have been long-time friends of Dave and Kai Ling. They had met in university and were inseparable during their schooling years. Eventually, the four friends became two couples. They settled in and began to enjoy their lunch.

“How was King Lear? The theatre show that you two caught last week?” Dave asked.

“Oh, it was splendid! There was an integration of hologram and live theatre elements that really transformed the experience. I am a fan of the traditional theatre—call me a purist, but it’s how I believe theatre should be. But this show convinced me of the possibility of bringing new elements in tactful and measured ways. Ask Joey. He loved it too,” said Alice.

“I mean the only reason why I ever watch theatre shows is because of Alice and yet I’m thoroughly engaged throughout the show. Absolutely delightful!” Joey chuckled.

“How are you able to find the time and head space for these things with the developments on the space colonisation front? How’s that coming along by the way?” Dave asked, teeming with excitement and eagerness.

“Well, my team and I are currently planning explorations in a newly discovered planet TOI-1231d and doing some expeditions on the planet to ascertain the suitability of the planet for colonisation," Joey replied. "I'm leading the team to do a series of on-site tests while packing samples to be further examined in the HQ."

"Speaking of that, I happen to know a think tank group on Space Exploration Ethics and know of someone in a separate project dedicated to working out the laws in these colonies," Kai Ling mentioned. "How is it practised on the ground? What is the attitude of the explorers when you are deciding on whether to colonise a planet? I personally have qualms about the term colonisation because of its bad reputation in history and baggage. It implies that we have the right to take over a certain space because of the assumption that we are somewhat superior to others—whatever lifeform that exists on that planet," Kai Ling continued. "We assume that we know more and better when we colonise and take over planets."

"In practice, we were taught two principles whenever we are out on expeditions. First, is to always harbour the attitude that we are learning from these spaces. It's about discovering and knowing what we don't know. Secondly, the colonies are not what the name suggest. In fact, I agree that the name 'colonies' have too much baggage. I am all for a change in the name. That can probably change the optics of what we do," Joey admits. "It is not perfect but at the basic level, we try our best to ensure that a newly discovered planet does not have lifeform."

"I think that space represents more than just the need for space—in fact there's no need for that because the population on earth is kept under strict control," Dave chimed in. "To me, space, like science, represents a frontier and a possibility. Not only physically but also psychologically. How else will we progress if not for that possibility of the tantalising unknown?"

"Space —" Joey said

"—is really that space of possibility in your psyche," Alice completed the sentence. "I can almost anticipate it every time," she said, rolling her eyes dismissively as she jested playfully. "It's like his mantra. He repeats it everywhere he goes; at every opportunity."

The group chuckled while Joey retreated in embarrassment at that comment. "All right. And that's my cue to stop talking about my work," said Joey. "Say, how are your plans for having a child coming along? Have you balloted for it?"

Kai Ling immediately eyed Dave sidelong, freezing up momentarily at the mention of the sensitive topic.

"We've planned a trip to the Infants Department so that Kai Ling can get a sense of what care for the child looks like," Dave answered firmly.

"Although, for me the other hurdle is understanding how the process of carrying a child can affect the mother psychological and emotionally," Kai Ling added.

"Ahh yes. The emotional attachment is real, I'll tell you," Alice said. "It is no doubt a magical feeling holding your child, even for a couple of minutes. Nine months of childbearing is not a short time. It's inevitable."

"How was that?" Kai Ling asked, "having to give up your child after all that time and having a visceral connection?"

"It's not easy. You have to prepare yourself for it. Bear in mind the real reason why you want to do it. The greater good is what will centre you throughout this whole process," Alice responded.

Kai Ling nodded sullenly. That was the narrative she knew in her head—the duty of the citizen. Alice has confirmed her fears of the experiences of mothers in the whole process. The question was whether the knowledge of the greater good can outweigh the instincts to be selfish. Dave looked at the dejected countenance of his wife, not being able to fully empathise but could visibly see how these considerations were exacting.

Registering her internal conflict, Alice reached her hand out to Kai Ling's and assured her, "I can't tell you that it'll be okay, but I can tell you that I'm here for you when the time comes. Shall we go on a trip? To the countryside? Maybe being in a different space would be good for you. When we're there we can chat as we unwind. I'll tell you everything you need to know without boring the boys."

"That sounds super. I think Kai Ling needs that," Dave said.

"Maybe you just need to be in a different environment to work out what you feel about this," Joey added.

Kai Ling nodded weakly. She was unresolved.

After Joey and Alice left, Dave turned to Kai Ling, held her hands and said, "I think we are lost in this process, so let's get more information to help us understand better." Something stabilised within Kai Ling with this gesture. Something stilled and she felt like maybe she could learn to tackle this decision a little more bravely.

***

It was the day of the visit. Kai Ling was up early. In fact, her eyes were wide open at four in the morning. She couldn't fall asleep thereafter. Mulling over the visit to the Infants Department that was coming up that day, it was impossible to still her mind. Sipping coffee in the living room on her own waiting for time to past.

Dave, on the other hand, was still fast asleep. At peace. Without worry. What a stark contrast to her unsettled emotions. Fear crept in, thrummed through her veins, and meandered through her heart. These episodes overwhelmed her, making her feeble inside and out. At that moment, the sound of the bedroom door opening snapped her out of her spiral. "How long have you been up?" Dave muttered as he ran his fingers through his asphalt-coloured hair.

"Just since 4 am," Kai Ling replied, listless with anxiety. Walking over to Kai Ling, he reached out to hold Kai Ling's hand. "It'll be fine," he whispered tenderly.

Looking into his sapphire eyes, Kai Ling knew that Dave did not fully grasp her crippling fear but that he was there, present. Kai Ling nodded slightly, acknowledging his presence.

"I'll get ready, grab a quick bite, then we can head off," Dave said.

As they departed from their apartment building, they each got onto their hoverboards. The soft and comforting glow of the sun filtering through the Dome warmed them up. The air was cool and crisp. They were travelling towards Calta, the civic centre of Zenkia Dome, that Dave and Kai Ling lived in. It was a 15-minute journey to the Infants Department, which was the regulatory body for all matters pertaining to child-bearing, pregnancy care, infant care, and also overseeing matters related to population control. Kai

Ling hardly spoke on the way there, mind fully occupied by what is to come.

After what seemed like an eternity to Kai Ling, the couple arrived at a tower that had an open garden at the middle floor of the entire building. The Infants Department's information centre was a place where prospective parents could ballot for the right to bear children for the State. Citizens did not have the free right to bear or raise children on their own—that right and responsibility laid with the State. All children after the age of one would have a Citizen Implant at the back of their spine just under the neck. The Implant was the link that uploaded all the data from the individual to the Core central system. Part of its function was to regulate some aspects of the physical condition such as regulating hormones so that fertilised embryos will be rejected by the body. In essence, women would not get pregnant if not pre-approved by the State.

****

> In the Pragmatic State, children are brought up by the State and parental relations are strictly forbidden. Kinship ties were identified as one of the root problems of hoarding and discriminatory behaviour that perpetuates inequality. Inheritance and generational accumulation of wealth, power and influence drive greed and result in the perpetual disparity of wealth, huge class gaps and even social injustice in society. As such, the Pragmatic State aims to eliminate this historical societal structure flaw to achieve true meritocracy and delivering same opportunities, resources, and rewards to all citizens.
>
> ⍰
>
> Pregnancies are under State control: Couples who wish to give birth will have to ballot for a chance within the quota. The State then allocates according to the couple's genetic profiling and achievements. Depending on population distribution analysis, the State tries to also maintain a significant portion of mixed racial, genetical differences, in order to have a healthy genetic pool diversity for mankind

survival. The wide range of genetic mix in the population has also effectively eradicated racial prejudice and discrimination. Once approved, the control within the body will create the optimal biological conditions to allow mothers to be pregnant.

At birth, the baby will be tagged at their wrists and ankles with the relevant information in the hospital. Thereafter they will be sent on a special railcar to the Capital city, Keb. Once they arrive at Keb, the identifier tags will be removed, leaving only the birth year. From there, all babies are deliberately mixed and dispatched to various care centres to be taken care of—mainly by robots with some human oversight. People only become unique individuals when they are one year old when they are issued their unique ID, a seven-digit alphanumeric code and name that is randomly generated for every baby. That is also the time they are implanted with the Citizen Implant.

****

As Dave and Kai Ling arrived at the Infants Department's visitor and information centre, they were immediately greeted and attended by a guide.

"Good morning you both! I'm Caleb and I'll be your guide and assistant for your time at the Infants Department today. How may I address the both of you? And how can I help you today?" said Caleb.

"We made an appointment at 10 am for the briefing to learn about the childbearing process and the nursery facilities. Under the names of Dave and Kai Ling," said Dave.

Swiping on the hologram projection emanating from his wristband, he began gesturing and swiping. "Ah, there we go. I've gotten your details. Perfect! I'm going to lead you to the waiting area. We'll just have to wait for another couple before we begin," Dave said. "Follow me."

Caleb led them through a long hallway with full length windows. Except for the cadences of their footsteps on the hard marble floor, the walk was silent. After ushering them into a room at the end of the hallway, Caleb said "I'll be with you in a moment. You can have a look at the documents that I'll be sending you through ECHO. While waiting, the materials will help you get a better understanding of the whole childbearing process in our society." Gesturing to a robot, Caleb said, "Rai can also prepare coffee and beverages should you need anything".

"Thanks very much, Caleb" Kai Ling said.

Kai Ling sat down, put on her visor, and started perusing the documents that were sent over by Caleb, while Dave busied himself with getting coffee from Rai. Soon after, Caleb returned to the room with another couple. A slightly plump man with dark skin and curly hair entered the room with a slender lady with dark brown eyes and obsidian hair.

"Hi Dave and Kai Ling, this couple will be joining us on the tour today. Meet Victor and Georgette," Caleb introduced. They exchanged the usual greetings and chatter, although Kai Ling was distracted.

"Are we all ready for the tour?" Caleb said with enthusiasm. "First of all, let me send out packages to all of you which will give you more details about our tour as well as some information sheet on childbearing, which I have already sent to Dave and Kai Ling." He gestured on his wristband. The rest of them automatically raised their wristbands to receive the information.

"The plan for today is to take you through four stops. Starting with your unique role in our society as a child bearer, followed by getting a fuller understanding of the experience of child-bearers, and how the State can support you during your pregnancy. We work closely with the internal department that looks at childbearing welfare, which you will find out more about. Finally, to cap off the visit, we will be taking you to a nursery to get an experience of how care for infants is given," Caleb continued. "With that, let's begin today's tour with an overall understanding of the role of the Infants Department, the State's policy of population control in the next room."

Caleb turned and began walking to another door in the waiting room that led to another room. There were seats in the dimly lit room and Caleb invited everyone to take a seat and to put on their visor to watch a ten-minute video. The video talked about the need to control population to regulate the use of resources but also to ensure that no one in the State had offspring. The video went on to describe the ills of having offspring and how that had historically resulted in disastrous consequences of income inequality and gross imbalance in the way wealth was distributed and hoarded.

This was what Kai Ling had known and talked about in the numerous committees she had been on. It was elementary, and yet, it felt different to be in the position of a potential child bearer and a recipient of that information. "It is absolutely necessary to ensure that the population is kept optimal to safeguard the sustainable use of resources... It is the duty of the citizen to perpetuate the human race. Prospective parents will have to ballot for the right to bear children and they will be notified within a month on their results."

Just as the video concluded, Caleb spoke, "Those are the fundamental principles upon which the State has organised its policy on childbearing. It is a critical process that is the foundation of how the society operates. At this point, does anyone have any questions before we move on to the next segment of the tour? Otherwise, you are free to ask me any question during the tour."

The group of four expressed that they did not have questions and decided to move on with the tour.

Entering the next room, the group was brought into a space with different interactive stations. "Here, we will be learning about the experience of the child bearer and how the Infants Department supports the child bearer during pregnancy. There is tremendous care, both physically and psycho-emotionally, that we strive to provide," Caleb said. "The State hopes to support all child bearers as much as possible because we understand the stresses that goes into childbearing. In this space, you will find different interactive stations that will initiate you into the process of childbearing. Please put on your visors as per the instructions at the stations."

Kai Ling started off with a station that articulated the pregnancy phase as well as the things that child bearers needed to look out for. Putting on her visor and activating the system with her wristband, a hologram appeared against the backdrop of a chart that articulated the pregnancy process. Her fears were confirmed. There were reports of child bearers developing emotional attachment during the pregnancy and post-natal depressions subsequently. The hologram talked about the support given to child bearers throughout their pregnancy such as courses with information on nutrition and well-being of the child bearer. In fact, their physiological changes were closely monitored by their Citizen Implants. When additional medical or psychological help is needed (when bodily stress was detected), the Medical Services will get in touch promptly and assign personnel to and assist the child-bearers. "Child-bearers will not be alone throughout their pregnancy. That is the State's promise to you," the hologram declared.

"That is true," Georgette chimed in uninvited. "I know of someone who had an emergency episode during her pregnancy. The medical support arrived within ten minutes."

"When it comes to psychological support, the Infants department offers support for the mental health of child bearers—" the hologram continued.

Turning to Georgette, Kai Ling asked, "What about anyone who might have suffered from postnatal depression? Do you know of anyone?"

"Well, I'm sure the State has got that covered, but I haven't known of anyone in that situation," Georgette said.

We all know there's support, but no one here has experienced it to be able to speak about it empathetically, Kai Ling thought.

"Perhaps I'll ask Caleb about it later when we regroup," Kai Ling replied.

Dave seemed to have left to visit another exhibit, leaving Kai Ling alone to wander. Moving on to another station, Kai Ling was greeted with an exhibit with a collection of objects sprawled on steel trays and tables infused with the clinical quality of a hospital.

"Put on your visor and pick up any object in this room. Each of them will tell you something about what the child bearing process is like and the resources available to child bearers on their journey," a voice from the speakers uttered as Kai Ling entered the room.

Kai Ling picked up an epidural needle. Immediately, a hologram visible to her through her visor created different texts and options surrounding the object. Clicking on "*History*", she learnt about the history of the epidural needle and how it was necessary to relief women of child labour pains. Kai Ling was given a walk through on child labour throughout history and how it has evolved. With technological advancement, the object was rendered obsolete. As Kai Ling foraged through the different objects available in the room, she felt like a detective uncovering clues to the mystery of pregnancy.

Eventually, Caleb regrouped everyone and wrapped up the session, "I hope everyone has had the chance to look through the exhibits and has walked away feeling better equipped about childbearing. Rest assured that the State has it all thought out. Feel free to ask me any questions along the way but for the next part of the tour, we will be travelling to Keb to visit the nursery where new-borns are brought to, taken care of and raised. We will be taking the hover rail to Keb in just a moment and a hovercar will be taking us to the station where we will transit to Keb."

A private hovercar picked them up from the visitor centre and dropped them off at Calta Station. From the gantry of the station, each of them passed through a gantry that was manned by a robot. There were multiple rail tracks heading in a different direction. The group darted for the hover rail that headed towards Keb. The hover rail unit they were on was white and slick. It levitated a couple of inches from the platform and stayed that way when the train took off. The journey to Keb took thirty minutes, during which passengers were served by robots if they wanted snacks or drinks.

In no time, they arrived at Keb and were immediately greeted by another hovercar that took them to the nursery facility. Entering the compound, they were greeted by a place that felt like a campus, peppered with luscious greenery in between throngs of buildings. Eventually, the hovercar stopped at a nondescript building that read "Arrival Centre".

Caleb brought the two couples through the side with special visitor access as part of Infants Department visits and took them to the Child Screening facility. He explained the process of how children are brought into the centre. The place was teeming with robots attending to the babies at a ratio of 1:1. Each robot held and tended to one baby as they came through in an orderly sequence. The robots with the babies were being examined individually to check on their health, which was then logged into the system. Babies were then tagged with their birth year after the checks were completed, removing all details of their genealogy. Thereafter, they were brought to visit the nursery for children aged 2-3 years old. There were more humans overseeing the children, with a Guider: robots: baby ratio of 1: 1: 8. According to Caleb, the number of Guiders taking care of babies increased with the age and the need for more psycho-emotional growth. They were then taken to visit facilities of children between the age of 10-12 years old, where they met a Guider, Anna. She was a petite lady with ginger coloured hair and emerald, green eyes. *She emanated bright energies*, Kai Ling thought.

"Hi everyone! I am Anna, the Guider of Nursery 23-13. Pleased to meet you!" Anna introduced. "Here at the 10-12-year-old hostel, Guiders provide support not just in physical care, but more importantly in emotional support for the children. We build a relationship and rapport with every child and live closely with them. Each group of Guiders takes care of 5 children. Our duties involve ensuring that the meals of the children are provided for, making sure that they attend school safely, supervising their leisure and play time, but most importantly supporting the children emotionally."

"You must really love kids in order to do this day and night isn't it?" Kai Ling asked.

"Well, I absolutely enjoy this. Truth is, I didn't always used to like kids. It was only until after I had given birth that I started to discover my maternal instincts," Anna elaborated. "Besides, children are wonderful! They teach me new things about the world every day. It's like interacting with people who will always have fresh perspectives and understandings of the world."

Kai Ling was piqued by the enthusiasm and passion that Anna spoke with. As the group continued moving on, Kai Ling continued speaking to Anna.

"You mentioned that you gave birth to two children. How was that process like?" Kai Ling asked.

"Terrifying, if I were to be honest," Anna answered without hesitation, then chuckled.

What a refreshingly candid reply, Kai Ling thought.

"The most terrifying part was the emotions that would have to be poured into the nine months of childbearing. The emotional attachment to the child is something that is real. Ask any child bearer and they'll tell you that is true," said Anna. "In fact, it was the experience that made me wanted to become a Guider. I had a lot of anxiety going into it. It also didn't seem like people understood where my concerns were—I mean it was frightening."

"That's exactly how I feel right now. Everyone is giving me either the 'correct' answers or they don't seem to empathise with my position or my fears," said Kai Ling.

"You're not alone! There were also a lot of questions that I had about the emotional connection that might come out of bearing a child for nine months. It's not a long time but it isn't short either. And if I were to be brutally honest, the bodily experience carrying the baby over nine months did something to my psyche. The maternal instincts that I had—wanting to nurture, protect and raise my child was there. I developed a strong desire to keep the baby."

"How did you manage that in the end?" Kai Ling enquired.

"Having to give my baby up was painful initially. I knew in my head that it was out of my duty to the State that I had to do this to begin with. But I couldn't reconcile that with my emotional desires. Eventually, I went for counselling and the possibility of channelling those emotions became possible through being a Guider," said Anna. "I was in the field of business management prior to childbirth. But after giving birth, I decided to try out being a Guider, and who knew it would stick for 5 years now! Seeing these kids, I feel the duty to treat them as my own—my daughter and son. As a result, I began treating all of them as my own," Anna added.

"That really helped you?" Kai Ling asked, half wondering if she, too, would feel the same if she was put in the same situation.

"Absolutely. I think that we don't recognise the impact that childbearing has on us as bearers. We have to recognise that these emotions are real. Being a Guider allowed me to channel my energies. I needed that and it stabilized me post-pregnancy. And more importantly, this experience has opened my eyes into recognizing that the love I have now for any child or elderly transcends the blood relationship. To me, it no longer matters how we are related to one another, but that society as a whole is many in one, and the love for others should also be as one."

Recognising that the emotions are real, Kai Ling thought. That was something that was not done enough and she was glad that Anna recognised it upfront.

"You're the first person who has been brave and forthcoming in explaining the issues surrounding pregnancy that are not spoken about. I'll bear these options in mind."

"I'm glad my own experience has been of help. Be brave Kai Ling. Know that there are outlets and channels available," Anna said, firmly and intently.

"I will be. And I have definitely taken up too much of your time! I better regroup with the rest," Kai Ling mentioned.

"Don't worry about it. It was my pleasure," Anna said.

As Kai Ling left to rejoin the group, which had gone on to the next segment of the tour, Anna walked away, out of view and as she entered a room, she disappeared right after the door closed.

***

Finally, it was the day of the road trip that the couples had been looking forward to. "Ready for the trip?" Alice asked glancing over at Kai Ling, eyes bright with anticipation as she made that comment.

"I'm really looking forward to having some time away from the Dome," Kai Ling replied. It was a long-awaited trip with Alice and Joey, and they were on the way to Reftet Station where they will take the rail out of the city.

Alice prattled on about what they could do when they arrive at the resort. Since the day at the Infants Department, Kai Ling could not stop mulling over what Anna shared. There was something inexplicable about the way Anna connected with her, a profundity that no one offered her when she voiced out her anxieties about childbearing. She needed space to consolidate what she had heard and getting out of the Dome might be just what she needed.

While on the hover rail, Kai Ling looked out the window and saw a Terraformer floating in the sky. These were huge facilities that was used to purify the planet surface as well as the air, making the Earth environment green and sustainable—this was the same technology used to terraform Moon, Mars, and other planets. This could only be achieved through huge advancement in science, and the uninterrupted effort of people in physical sciences and societal structure development. Without the need to care for the old or young in a family setting, every individual is thus able to develop to their fullest potential thereby fulfilling the three mottos. She knew that the underlying need for her to bear a child stemmed from the foundations of the society.

From Reftet Station they eventually arrived at Lubar Station, got onto a hovercar and drove towards a coastal town, Gordon, with approximately 100 houses and a small town centre. Private companies own resort towns in the countryside which could be rented by citizens—everyone in the society was given an allowance to spend on countryside visits and holidays. However, those who were able to afford it had the option of purchasing a countryside house from private companies. Houses were built in a similar fashion. Dave owned a cosy cabin in Gordon, developed by Ceres Corporation, that was perched on a cliff overlooking the sea. Ceres Corporation was known to develop projects that had a touch of history and rustic charm that appealed to the sensibilities of Kai Ling. "It's reminiscent of the Scottish towns," she would always say.

Hopping onto the hovercar, Dave immediately commanded ECHO to play the music from the 1970s—AC/DC and started driving. When it came to music for the road, Dave was an old soul. There was a kick in music that was somehow befitting of a road trip. The journey of the countryside was something that Dave thoroughly enjoyed. The road trip was part of the experience because within the main Dome, there would be no opportunity to commute for an extended period of time.

As they drove through the winding road, they were greeted by overgrown wilderness, sprawling scrubs and bushes, and the speckled hues of mustard, sunburst orange and scarlet red. The countryside was a refreshing contrast from the experience of the city, the organisation followed the order of nature. Manually driving on the road was one of Dave's favourite things to do—it was one of the rare and occasional pleasures that one could not get within the Domes. He enjoyed winding through the undulating roads and taking in the landscape that they were driving through.

The areas near the Dome consisted of grassland, not full-fledged forests. Animals roamed freely in the grassland—various species of deer, foxes, lemmings, and rabbits sprint freely among shrubs. To keep people safe, there were drones that patrolled the countryside, keeping the designated township safe by monitoring the movement of the predatory animals, driving them out whenever they came too close to the town.

After they had finally settled into the cabin, it was already late afternoon. They decided to cook and prepare for a barbeque dinner out in the yard. While robots were available in assisting humans in the preparation of food, the four of them decided to do it themselves—perhaps in keeping with the experience of being out for vacation.

"You seem happier, Kai Ling," Alice commented as she and Kai Ling were preparing the ingredients for the barbeque. "How was the visit to the Infants Department?"

"Do I? The visit was eye-opening. I met someone. She was a Guider who took us around the facility at Keb," Kai Ling replied. "I connected to her deeply... having gave birth twice, she shared rather honestly about her experience of being a child bearer having to manage the emotions and attachments that developed when surrendering the child to the State. And for her, becoming a Guider was one of the ways that helped her cope with that. Did you have that experience too when you gave birth?"

"Absolutely," Alice replied. "At that moment of giving my first child up, I remember feeling that pang of loss and recalcitrance. During the nine months of pregnancy, it is impossible not to develop the sense of attachment to the baby that is growing within you. If you remember, for 2 years, I served as a Guider after my first child. I too, met someone who could relate to my anxiety, fears, and pain. Come to think of it, I am indebted to that person for the candid sharing of her experience. I think her name was Sarah. I met her at the hospital by chance and she was sharing her experience of giving birth to the child for the fourth time and encouraging me to consider the option of being a Guider."

"Ahh yes. I remember that period. You didn't really say very much back then. About that decision," Kai Ling replied.

"There was a lot going on—emotionally, mentally and physically. I don't think I was in a position to share too deeply. But in retrospect, I think the State provided the necessary support for me to tide myself through that period. It did get much easier after I became a Guider. I was able to manage my second pregnancy better afterwards," Alice paused midway as she was chopping up the vegetables, deep in thought as if she was reflecting to herself. "Strange as this sounds, perhaps a part of me still appreciates that I could undergo this deeply human experience. Painful, no doubt. But it was both painful and beautiful in a way. Men will never get the chance to understand the profound attachments and development of maternal instincts," said Alice with a tone of levity, shooting Kai Ling a short wink.

An exclusive experience of being human, thought Kai Ling. *Was this what Anna experienced too? She has never thought of it that way but that put things into perspective.*

"If I approached this individualistically, I am not sure how child-bearing value-add to my life. But as a citizen, it is my duty to go through with it for the perpetuation of mankind," Kai Ling said, as if to conclude her internal thought process.

It dawned on Kai Ling that there was something quite poetic about having this conversation with Alice while preparing the food for the barbeque personally, without the help of robotics. It was in that moment that it all came together for her—there was something about the human experience that she could get behind.

Having heard from Anna and now from Alice, her bravery grew stronger. "The most important thing is first to recognise that these feelings are real and part of the childbearing experience," Alice emphasised. "The State recognises this too, I think. And perhaps that is just the way it is—the experience of carrying and worrying for a child is not something that can or should be 'solved'."

They continued preparing food for the evening, chattering away at anything and everything. Something came together that evening for Kai Ling. The feelings of anxieties persisted, no doubt. However, there were available channels for people to manage that experience. And yet in that tension and pain, lies a human experience to be gained—in the same way preparing food personally or driving along a meandering road in the countryside could bring.

Samir 1Z08Q36

The Entrepreneur

The sound of the rain prattled on as the wind howled. With a pensiveness Samir always adorned, he sat reclined in his chair, left hand swirling a glass of whisky. There was a stately air to his presence. He was fair skinned with light brown hair, thin and deceptively petite for someone with the stature of a business owner. It was 7 pm. His office was minimal and clean, much like his home. That his space in the office mirrored the space he had at home was unsurprising—lines between work and life were synonymous. There was no distinction between those categories. Devoted to his career and calling, he never settled down with anyone. It was a fact that he knew, that he was occasionally reminded of.

He owned Sprint Industries, a leading company in robotics that had grown into a conglomerate, which also dabbled in the design of space components and a research centre for all kinds of sciences. It was a prolonged day at work—every day was. Samir lived and breathed every moment of his work. A meticulous and precise person, he personally saw to every matter or issue that surfaced in a day. His robotics company was the leading company in the manufacturing, research and design of robotics that permeated daily life. With Sprint Industries' robots, he eliminated all forms of manual labour and unsafe work.

Being one of the pioneers in the Pragmatic State at 120 years old, Samir was one of the earliest pioneers who had seen the transformation of the Pragmatic society. Sprint Industries was one of the pioneers in the field of Robotics that made possible the replacement of hackneyed methods of industrial production, manual work, agriculture, law enforcement, household living and personal care among many others. By harnessing technology to eliminate the need for labour, the robotics industries transformed the structure of economic activity and the way people approach work.

�

Samir was waiting for his managers to return from dinner for the group strategy meeting, 'War room sessions' as Samir called it, where they will work on the continuous development of his company. War room sessions usually happened after office hours, stretching late into the night. They were charting out the growth areas that could be possible for Sprint Industries—the sectors they should focus on that could yield the highest returns, not in terms of profits but in terms of the research potential, the breadth of growth and the positive impact that it could bring for the society. Discussions on vision and forecasting were not merely focusing on the immediate year or two but the future decades of human progress. His train of thoughts was disrupted by quick, impatient knocks on the door. Judging from the cadence of the knocks, Samir knew it had to be Freddy from Marketing and Consumer.

"Come in."

The door opened and Freddy glided through the door and headed straight to the meeting table opposite Samir's desk. He had a glib tongue and was smooth with his words—the way you would expect of someone who knows his audiences well and would always tailor to them. "Hi Samir, how's it going? Had your dinner?" Freddy twittered.

"Just having a quick drink for now," said Samir.

"Alcohol for dinner! Sounds splendid," Freddy responded, "I'll leave you to it and get ready for the meeting."

�

As the heads of departments streamed in, they exchanged the usual greetings and chatter. Banter filled Samir's office as more of them arrived and settled in.

"Everyone is here. Shall we begin? Let's hear what you guys have to say" Samir said, culling the conversations in the room.

�

Paul got the ball rolling. As Head of Products, he presented the company's last quarterly figures. Sprint Industries did fairly well in the main consumer robotics market and maintained a solid hold on their market dominance. The recent rollout of a new library of "Techniques" meant that now most home-based robots could perform duties like experts in cooking, carpentry and housework based on the uploaded knowledge of experts in various fields. Anyone with the know-how in any aspect could upload and share their knowledge on particular fields of work and earn IP rights. The team of engineers at Sprint Industries then turned the knowledge into codes and algorithms that became options that consumers could choose for their robots.

"With the concept of Techniques subscriptions, we have been able to create individualised robots that catered to the specific needs of individuals.' Paul asserted. "Contributions to the Techniques Library has encouraged innovation that surpasses what is possible with the pool of workers at Sprint Industries. By modernising and proliferating these skills, Sprint has raised the quality of living for the general population. Content is the new product that we are selling," Paul concluded. "To me, the strategy would be to focus on the consumer market and grow the capabilities of our technology through consumer-led demand."

Lionel, the Head of Technology was up next. He talked about the research on the competitors in the field of Nano-robots. Beginning his report with conviction, he said, "Hitherto, Nano-robots have been used mainly in the medical field through insertion into the human body for recovery, monitoring or medical procedures. However, the new remote recharging technology could be the next quantum leap in this sector. This field is where we want to concentrate our energies and focus our operations. Pace Corporations and Sprint have been talking over the past couple of months about the possibility of an acquisition. We're exploring the potential merger of technologies, which is a potential growth area because we will now be harnessing the business potential of combining these two technologies," Lionel said, brimming with excitement. "Imagine what happens when the best minds come together to invent and design the next cutting-edge product!"

"I disagree and I'll tell you why," Joel interjected. "The next growth potential lies in partnerships with the State." Lionel looked dismayed to have his presentation interrupted, although he was done with his segment of the presentation.

"Look, the State is the steadiest investor of all." Joel asserted, "We've been co-funding with the State for years now. The research areas are yielding results in the next-generation propulsion system which would be implemented on their own but could have ground-breaking implications in the field of space exploration." Joel was the Head of State Partnerships working closely with the State in developing research in the areas identified by the State. "Considering how space exploration is the next frontier of humankind, it is almost an imperative to devote resources to move Sprint towards a new territory," Joel argued.

Everyone seemed to be proposing markedly different areas of growth. Tensions grew with the presentation of different perspectives that the heads represented. Samir was silent. Poker face. Although everyone knew that he was taking in the information and processing every proposition with the utmost criticality. Amidst the grunts and gestures of impatience, Freddy flamboyantly jumps in to push for an interstellar focus.

"Precisely that, Joel. I think we ought to expand and generate a continuous stream for our space programme," Freddy asserted. "In fact, my contact in Defence Services is looking for a new generation of shield technology to be used in large area coverage protection in space missions. That's a project with gargantuan returns if we can get it off the ground with them. It would no doubt propel the business and generate unprecedented profits for the company!" Freddy exclaimed.

Amidst the storm that was raging in the room, Gerard, the Deputy CEO and right-hand man of Samir sat unfazed and unperturbed by the anxious debate that unveiled in the room. He was younger than Samir, although he was well-advanced in his age. He has been with the company since the beginning and knows what Samir looks out for. During the meeting, he occasionally cast glances at Samir, shrugging in agreement with Samir at some befuddling assertions.

"I think," Gerard spoke unhurriedly, curbing the noise that was in the room, "we have got to ask ourselves where the impact lies. We are too absorbed in the current potential of what you are facing in your different sphere. We need to be less opportunistic and reactionary. Instead, we ought to take a step back to withdraw ourselves from the immediacy of the potential. All of you are missing the one thing that matters the most. Long-term impact. That is what is truly 'profitable'," Gerard concluded.

At that mention, Samir nodded—the first indication of his response throughout the whole meeting. "Gerard speaks my mind. What everyone has proposed so far is not cutting it. These are superficial analysis of the market and near-term projections," Samir finally spoke.

Everyone stood in anticipation of the incisive analysis that Samir always gave. "None of the areas identified are as ground-breaking as you think they are," Samir said unreservedly. He was not one to sugar-coat the hard truths. "What I expect to hear are directions that have direct and long-term benefits to people's lives. Don't get caught up with the present opportunities. You need to look passed it all to identify where value lies. What Paul mentioned about the consumer market and the involvement of individuals and experts to contribute to a "Techniques" bank is certainly something to look into. I also concur that an interstellar focus would be beneficial in the long-term. Those were good suggestions with a misplaced focus. Pay attention, not only to profits, but impact." His words sank in, ceasing the crossfires and incisively synthesized the ideas that we in the room. There was balance in the room again. He was a man of few words, but when he did speak, his terse words were always penetratingly accurate, calculated and purposeful.

How will I find my successor? What will happen after I'm gone? he asked himself. That had been a question that has been weighing on his mind. He had begun thinking about his potential successor and started making provisions. At the moment, there was no one except Gerard who was capable of fully grasping his vision and ideals. Samir wanted his company to be a force for good—one that was hinged upon the right motivations and principles. Belonging to the same generation as Samir, Gerard was not the ideal successor.

"Have a think about what I said and let's reconvene when everyone is ready with a fresh proposal next Wednesday," Samir announced.

One by one, his subordinates slowly left, and he was finally left alone. Time to head home for the night. Packing up, he slowly made his way out of the building. The night always seemed the loneliest. There was something about darkness that amplified the disquiet in him. As the world whizzed past and the moon gazing down at him, he wondered about his achievements throughout life. He hated not being at work. *In this life, has he done enough?* he thought to himself. *But enough for what? Himself or the society?* In ploughing his time into his business, Samir sacrificed his own relationships. Every decision had its trade-offs. Though he was cognizant of it, it never failed to leave a bitter aftertaste. On one hand, he was completely aware of what he was choosing, and yet, these moments of reflection got to him. Perhaps it was the therapeutic drone of the raindrops that made a good background for reflection.

The fifteen-minute commute home felt much longer because of the drone of his inner voice. Arriving at his mansion, he breathed in the crisp laundered scents of his garden. The smell ushered in a different cadence. For someone who owned a lavish business, his home was surprisingly modest, though it was no doubt fitted with the latest technology that had not been released in the market.

"Get the bath ready," he got off his hovercar. He glided across the hallway and into his bedroom. His house was designed with earthy tones, textured by wood, and padded by soft curves in the architecture and the furniture selection. He was never after the money in the business, which the simple design illuminated.

All freshened up, he retreated into his bedroom and sank into his bed. It always hit him in the dead of night. Save for his own breathing and the sound of the crickets, the house was dead quiet, amplifying the loudness of his loneliness. Pushing that thought out of his mind, he reiterated to himself that as long as he made his life worthwhile, contributing meaningfully to society, he would be fine. Filling his mind up with work again, he found the equilibrium. Gradually, he drifted into sleep.

****

The State is the controller of most resources. Owning the majority of economic assets, the State is able to fund a lot of social programs. Functions that are determined to be basic human rights sat squarely within the domain of the State and are exclusively driven and funded by State.

Basic to tertiary education was offered to every citizen in the Pragmatic State, which is the basis for a fair society where everyone got access to education. To move around, every citizen is also given a stipend to purchase a hoverboard, maintain and upkeep it. When it comes to healthcare, all citizens had access to hospitalisation and outpatient treatments. However, any upgrades to the ward or choices in the grade of medical equipment and technology beyond what was determined to be the basic treatment would require citizens to bear their own cost.

These are public goods that are believed to be essential. On the other hand, the private sector drives most of the innovation in society, such as research centres and special healthcare.

The economy is driven by ideas rather than production, and robotics had been key in this transformation. Robots and energy are unlimited and free, which means that robots did most of the heavy lifting when it comes to manual and physical work. Most of the economic activities in the Pragmatic State are in research, development, and the improvement of processes and products. Content and skills creation is the linchpin of the economy. Original content and programmes are uploaded to robots so that everyone can benefit from them. The creator gets the Intellectual Property Rights.

The emphasis on technology as the main economic activity improves the quality of life. Robots such as those created by Sprint Industries is the backbone of much of how society functions. Consumer robotics elevated and altered the mode of daily living. Integrated AI systems are also incorporated within building design to optimise systems and operations.

�

****

�

Samir opened his eyes as he noticed the shaft of light that invited itself into his bedroom, exposing the swirls of dust floating in mid-air. The ceiling was white. The morning chirping sound of the birds outside the window was his daily alarm. Wednesday. *Site visit to the production factory today*, he recalled. He had a deluge of appointments and meetings, but he was not one to forget a single detail. Having a packed schedule was exhilarating to him because it made every day feel like a new challenge.

Reaching out to his ECHO wristband on the side of his bed, he said "Retrieve schedule for today. What is the first thing I am doing today?"

"Site visit at Helper Robots factory," ECHO replied, confirming his internal calendar.

�

Samir made it a point to walk the ground physically, not just in a virtual environment from the visor. He was old school in that way. He believed in the importance of understanding operations on the ground and being able to connect it to the overarching strategies of the company. With the new launch of the Helper Robots looming around the corner, the Products department was in crunch time of reviewing the products before the product launch. Almost every household in society was fitted with one of Sprint Industries' products. The Helper Robots were an update on the existing Helpers. Sprint Industries was in the business of perfecting machine learning and the AI's ability to personalise and predict behaviour of their users to tailor to their needs. They were modifying the prototype of a Helper that was able to pre-empt the needs of their users over time, catering to routines, habits, interests, and age of the user. With his team, Samir was looking at a programme update.

�

Well-liked and well-respected, Samir was always welcomed by his subordinates. There were no airs about him—he never pulled rank and treated all his workers with equality, dignity and respect.

“Good to see you today, Mr. Samir,” Jonas, the Operations Director of the production site greeted Samir as he entered. Samir was early for the meeting with the team in charge of the new launch.

“It’s a beautiful morning, isn’t it?” Samir said gazing at the shaft of morning light filtering through the translucent ceiling of his factory. “How have things been? You’ve had time to catch a breather given the craziness of the period?”

“Here and there. Pretty much!” Jonas replied. “And you?”

“Ahh, breathers. Well, I take them when I’m having my meals!” Samir chuckled. “I suppose there’s no need for breathers when you’re breathing every moment isn’t it?” Samir winked.

As the Helper Robots were slated to be released in a couple of months, Samir increased the frequency of his visits to the production site to once per week. During these meetings, the team would update on the figures in the research and development of the products.

When the team eventually convened in the meeting room at the factory, they gave a quick rundown of the status of PersonCare 2.0 of the Helper Robots. He was sharp, observant, and meticulous about details that were provided, yet at the same time, he was incredibly forgiving about mistakes. Though Samir might be ruthlessly candid in catching people’s bluff or pointing out their mistakes, his comments were always constructive and focused on how one could rectify the mistake from thereon. When Jensen made a mistake during the meeting with the figures that he reported on, Samir did not hesitate to call it out. He never bothered to embellish his words with euphemisms—he cut to the chase and struck at the heart of the matter.

“Don’t mind that I pointed your mistake straight-up, Jensen. It’s better to realise that you made a minor error upstream than to solve an amplified problem downstream. Work at it and you’ll be fine,” Samir asserted.

“I hear you, Mr. Samir. I’ll be more cautious the next time,” Jensen replied.

His life revolved around his business. His subordinates were his closest companions by virtue of the sheer amount of time he spent on his business. Everyone knew what Samir was like. While he was a strict boss, he was never unreasonable. He would never hesitate to catch anyone's bluff, but one can be sure that it was never personal and that it was always justified.

***

Wrapping up his meeting at the factory, he took his leave and made his way to Zanda district where Marvin and Kate resided. They lived in a private estate in a serene neighbourhood and a couple of them were having a regular get-together over lunch. It took Samir about twenty minutes on his personal hoverboard—a prototype edition that was not out in the market. He would be the first to test out any product before they were released into the market. Sandra, Cheryl, Marvin and Samir had been long-time friends since their university days. Marvin was a medical researcher. He always had the flair and inclination towards medical research and that was how he got to know Kate who was a biomedical scientist.

"Samir! You're finally here. We started without you because our tummies were growling incessantly," Sandra exclaimed upon Samir's arrival at the apartment.

"You have got to come try the steak that Marvin made. It's exquisite!" Cheryl chimed in. "Please invite us over more often. I have missed your cooking!"

"I'm glad you're relishing it! That makes me absolutely pleased," Marvin exclaimed.

"Know that you are welcome to our place any time... How's your book coming along, Cheryl?" Kate asked.

"It has come a long way! I was in a little bit of a writer's block earlier this year. I couldn't write. Nothing flowed. Things have gotten better after I decided to change up my environment and exposed myself to other contexts a little more. It takes something wholly different to jolt you and to create pathways that can lead you to think more creatively." Cheryl replied.

"I love that you are doing what you've always excelled in, Cheryl," said Samir. "By the way, you have been living in the Elders

District for more than a year now since Albert passed. How did you find it so far?"

"To be frank I'm loving it more than initially thought. Aside from my robotic helper Javier taking charge of household chores and physical care of me, I'm now making a lot more friends with neighbours of our age and we are a tightly knitted community taking care of each other, especially on an emotional level." Cheryl elaborated.

A sense of comfort settled into Samir, knowing that Cheryl is well taken care of and in good company. "I'm glad to hear that."

"It's funny how we are where we're at today isn't it?" Sandra added. "We've lived for more than a century now. Witness how we have each explored our various interests from ground zero... I mean, look at Samir! Who knew that geek of a boy with his rounded glasses would live to become an industry leader?" Sandra roared cheekily as the rest broke out into a burst of riotous laughter.

"I'm glad we're all right where we're supposed to be. With my experience, I have been mentoring other civil servants on policy planning. All of us here are in some ways consultants. Quite frankly, don't you think the society is milking us for every last buck?" Sandra joked. At 120 years old, Sandra was still the same Sandra as back in university. Candid, unabashed and straightforward.

"Enough with your nonsense, Sandra," Samir spoke with a deep, gruff voice. "I think we followed our intuitions to pursue what made the most sense and meaning to each of us. Regardless of what we chose, there was flexibility in the system to accommodate us and allow us to pursue arête in this life."

They continued catching up with one another and updating each other on the endeavours that they were each embarking on. *We are where we are because of our disposition, talents, and strengths but also our decisions. What would my alternate life be? What would I do if I had not chosen to labour at work?* Samir thought to himself. As the luncheon came to a close, they bid their goodbyes while Samir wondered about how his path might look like if he was born with a different disposition and had chosen a different life for himself. He had a nagging curiosity about what could be.

He rushed back home because he had an appointment with his lawyer. They met monthly to settle the tax and reporting matters related to his company. However, recently, he began to think about his assets and how he would want his company to be led. Knowing that after he died, the State will take over the ownership of his corporation, he was eager to pave the way for the best candidate to continue running the company and making executive decisions. Shortly after he arrived back home, Graham and his team of assistant lawyers came by.

"How's it going, Samir," said Graham, calm and stoic as usual.

"All good today. I had a luncheon with some old friends at their apartment and had just returned home not too long before you arrived, "Samir said as they walked down the hallway towards Samir's home office.

⍰

According to the law, every item and belongings that exists are tracked by the Core system to ensure ownership of assets is not passed between individuals, not even to their spouses except in some obscure circumstances. The bigger problem for Samir was who will run the company when he was gone. While he created and birthed his company, the State will eventually come to own it. Samir knew that when that time comes, the State will not be running the business. That was the primary reason why he brought Graham and his team in.

"Thank you for coming, Graham," said Samir, "Have you been waiting long?"

"Hi Samir, not at all," Graham replied. "How can I help you today?"

"I've been giving it some thought. I'm well-advanced into the golden years of my life and I know that the government will be taking over all the assets after I'm gone. When that happens, I need to make sure that there is a management team that is in place to succeed and run the company," said Samir. "With the foundations involved in co-funding for science, Gerard has already been placed as the trustee. I would like to appoint someone else for the company."

"I see. Let's get cracking in terms of ensuring that your assets are properly allocated then. With the number of assets you have, this is going to take a while," Graham responded.

"For now, I have Paul in mind for the position. He is empathetic and always looking at the betterment of people's lives. Although he isn't quite the perfect candidate, he's the best I've got at the moment. As to where my funds will go, I'd like to explore investing in the arts or social affairs. All my life, the way I've learnt to impact other people is through technology and profits. Now, I would like to be more concerted and deliberate in channelling my personal resources to the underfunded sectors. Would you help to work out the legal aspect of those projects?" Samir asked.

They spent the rest of the day working out the finer details of Samir's plans. It was important for Samir to leave his mark. He wanted to make sure that the good work that has been done thus far will not end with him leaving the world. This continuity was important for him.

****

> Personal income tax is a progressive tiered structure to prevent hoarding. Above a minimum income threshold, the lowest bracket taxed at 10% and highest level up to 75%. Due to the abundance of resources, individuals are not driven for the accumulation of personal wealth but accomplishments to better society and living. Money and its pursuit are viewed and perceived differently in the Pragmatic State as citizens do not require it for survival, but for additional consumption and expenditure.
>
> A high level of surveillance and transparency in ownership of assets, transfer of funds in the banking system and declaration of taxation are maintained by AI systems.
>
> Private sector corporations are still the key drivers of production and efficient allocation of resources; hiring of manpower.
>
> When someone passes on, the State will take over all ownership of assets. Individuals are seen only as temporary custodians and developers of resources and assets, based on

the logic of the three mottos. During their lifetime, they are entitled to amass personal wealth and enjoy the fruits of the labour which they accumulate through hard work, entrepreneurship, tenacity, and capabilities. This enables true meritocracy and mirror the physical reality that people come into the world with nothing and will leave the world taking away nothing.

In the case of a company, the State will own the shares in the company—although the existing management team will continue to run the company. The State will likely sell the stakes in the public market to enable the new generation to benefit from the economic yields. State taking over inheritance is a very efficient allocation of resources within the living population/generation as it prevents hoarding and unfair allocation of resources. Without the passing down of wealth to the next generation, everyone is entitled to the same starting point in life and development opportunities.

****

***

"Prepare breakfast," Samir commanded ECHO as he woke up in the morning—the first thing he always did. The sun was not up yet. He was used to being up before everyone else was. Shuffling out of bed, he went about his usual routine. Even as he was going about his usual routine his mind ran like clockwork—drifting in from his investment plans to his company's overall strategy. He consumed and devoured his work every waking moment.

"What's my schedule like today?" he asked.

"You have a full schedule with a small window from 11 am to 12 noon. The first meeting begins at the headquarters with a potential investor in the Helper Robot technology at 9 am," ECHO replied steadfastly.

"A window. Schedule a meeting with Nicholas during that window then. The agenda would be to discuss the decisions made at the strategy meeting," Samir commanded.

He nibbled his avocado toast half-heartedly, scrolling his interface for the daily business news. "Maverick Technology breaks new ground with their consumer line of robots that have new automated systems," he read. His mind sprang into action, thinking about the implications of the news and how he should be making tweaks and changes vis-a-vis this change. He was reaching out for his interface and rolled out the keyboard at the dining table. It was his usual routine to work after breakfast after getting caught up with the news over breakfast. He was religiously routine and followed his systems to the letter. After all, he believed that designing systems was a craft—they help to organise what would otherwise be loose and separate. It takes a keen eye to identify issues and devise creative solutions. He took out his interface and rolled out the keyboard, only to be dismayed by an error message that showed up on the hologram:

"Unable to connect to Sprint Industries integrated system."

⍰

Turning to ECHO, he summoned Max, the IT robot that helped to maintain the systems and operations at home, he asked, "Run diagnostics to identify the problem." Within seconds, he was informed by Max, "Connection to Sprint Industries network broken. Rectifying now. Estimated time of resolution—2 hours." He tried several ways to troubleshoot but it seemed like he just needed to let the system run its own programme to rectify the issues. With time on his hands, he began to panic about what he should do. The worry was not about the data and the operations—he had perfectly competent subordinates whom he had the full trust would run the business just fine in his absence. He was more fearful of solitude. He was never free and would fill his schedule without a break every day. He tried to shrug it off and intuitively decided to take a walk.

He felt himself being pulled by a different rhythm and imperative—he began thinking about his own time on earth—the life that he has led and the legacy that he was leaving behind. He walked without a destination in mind, following where his body was leading him. Being packed was the cadence that he was so used to all his life. Instinctively, he headed towards the city centre. It did not occur to him that he could have gotten on his hoverboard. Although he would not have known what destination to head towards.

Walking along, he became cognisant of the quietness that surrounded him. He lived far from the city centre. Alone on the wide pavement of his district with not a soul in sight, it hit him. How did he find himself alone? There was no one he could turn to but the sound of the wind and the touch of the sun.

Having ploughed his entire life into delivering impact to society through robotics and technology, he never quite had the time to develop strong relationships with anyone, let alone a partner. The friendship support networks that the government put in place never interested him. Work was everything. Regardless of how impactful his work was, Samir knew that he gave up relationships and intimacy because of his enchantment with business and impact. He was aware of the trade-off. Or so he thought. It would come as the occasional wave of loneliness or bouts of regret, but there was never really any time for him to entertain those thoughts or feel those emotions. That day, without access to work, which was the ballast that anchored him, the trade-offs that he was able to shelve became illuminated.

Absorbed, he did not realise his thoughts and his subconscious body led him to a park. Wearily, he rested on the bench in the park. He stole a glance at ECHO. Only thirty minutes had passed. Meandering in his mind palace felt much longer. *Was it all worth it? Have I impacted enough people to warrant the sacrifices that I've made in my life? What if that sacrifice amounted to nothing? Have I done enough in bringing about the impact to justify what I gave up?*

Against the morning sun, he squinted at the sight of an elderly figure approaching him.

"A warm and lovely day, isn't it?" the man remarked, "Can I take a seat here?" The appearance of this unknown stranger snapped him out of his spiral.

"Absolutely," Samir replied.

"I'm Elliot. You?" Elliot introduced.

"Samir," Samir muttered.

"Oh? Samir? You do look familiar... Samir of the Sprint Industries? What a pleasure to meet you in person!" Elliot exclaimed, "I didn't know that you live in this district."

Samir felt his spirits being uplifted by the infectious energy of this stranger who was comfortable in his own skin. Grounded. Anchored. "Today is special. You wouldn't find me here on any other day," Samir admitted.

"Then I must be in luck! To be bumping into the owner of Sprint Industries on an unassuming weekday morning!" Elliot grinned.

"Something came up and I had some free time on hand. Without anything to do, I had somehow ended up here. It was a strange journey. I've never had so much time to my thoughts... It became apparent to me that I was completely alone—literally and figuratively. I started thinking about whether everything I have done so far was worth it," Samir rambled.

"I'm alone too—literally and figuratively," Elliot chimed, "You know, I have thought about these things that you're grappling with currently." Samir perked up, intrigued at the mention of it. Elliot continued, "I spent my life strategising, developing, and building an infrastructure for the People's Networks (PN). You know how pivotal friendships are in our society. The PN is incredibly vital for emotional and social support in our society. Like you, I am alone. I have poured everything I had into developing the PN, which compromised my relationships. There's still much to be done but these Networks are important anchors for people. I spent all my waking moments refining the PN and making sure that the organisation worked better. But at the end of the day, I was fully aware of the fact that I was alone. But I soon realised that if I chose this path, I would have to bear the responsibility for this decision. There will always be trade-offs, Samir. But first, it's important to acknowledge that those emotions exist and will continue to exist."

"I think we're similar in many ways, Elliot. You and I, we're both working on different aspects of the human condition and striving to improve our time on earth. While you work in the emotional realm, I have been labouring to improve the physical comfort and ease of people. As you were speaking, I am wondering if there are synergies in the work that we do. Imagine if we merged our business functions. What would that look like?" Samir described, lost in his thoughts and ideas. "What would scaling up look like for something like this?"

"That is an interesting proposition. There could be ways to do this. But tell me, have you attended any of the PN activities?"

"No, I haven't," Samir replied. "My support network came from the long-time friends that I've known for years. If I were to be perfectly candid, a part of me always knew that I longed for someone. I think it's normal too. Isn't it? But I've never dared to acknowledge or confront that fact."

"To come to terms with it, you have to acknowledge those emotions, or you'll never get past that knot."

Acknowledge those emotions. That struck a chord. Perhaps he has been engaging the issue with his brain more than his heart all this while. Somehow, Samir found Elliot's viewpoints extremely wise and enlightening even though they are of similar age.

"That is perhaps the duality of the human condition that no technology can solve," Elliot mused, "and perhaps that is for the best. There is something quite sublime about the duality of things that co-exists. Tensions reveal hearts in strife, which is not necessarily a bad thing. A heart that is in strife is also a heart that's alive." The poetic words resounded.

"Are you at peace with your decisions now?" Samir asked.

"If being at peace means being able to acknowledge and manage those emotions when they arise, then yes," Elliot said, with a slight chuckle and gentleness. "You see. There will be trade-offs in any decision you make. The important thing is to recognise that the different pathways lead you to different destinations, and no path will be perfect. Be aware of the place where you are truly actualising."

Samir was enthralled by the words of Elliot. Something about his words anchored him.

"Thank you for your words. Before today, I haven't needed to confront what I had always been pondering about."

"Well, I am glad my experience was of some good to another person!" Elliot replied.

Samir snuck a glance at his watch. If he began walking back home now, he would arrive home just when the connection is restored.

As if he was replying to Samir's thoughts, Elliot immediately announced, "I've taken up enough of your time today and I should go. It was such a pleasure talking to you Samir. May our paths cross again."

Getting up to leave, the two men headed in the opposite direction. The lacklustre energy that Samir came to the park with slowly dissipated. He now knew exactly what his lot was. It was serendipitous that he got to meet Elliot. He needed that conversation to help him find a way forward. Turning back to look at Elliot who was walking away, he felt his heart swell with gratitude. Elliot strolled away from Samir, and when he got out of Samir's view, his body began to slowly vanish.

Takahashi K2L97P0 and Eva 4S234W0

The Leaders

"How are the Domes doing in terms of resource allocation?" Takahashi asked his subordinates.

"The number of resources available vis-à-vis the population growth rate is healthy. However, there are some Domes, such as Sombrero and Circinus that have maxed out on their allocated resources," Jeremy, his subordinate answered.

"What is the contribution rate like in those Domes? It's a good indicator of whether the people in the Dome are contributing to the various aspects of the system," said Takahashi.

Toggling with the chart filters on his hologram projection, Jeremy responded, "According to the indicator, it appears that the contribution rate in those Domes were indeed lower. They are not producing work or contributing to the growth of the society as efficiently." Takahashi face tightened, creases forming across his dark brown skin. Pursing his lips, he said, "That's a sweeping statement. Be mindful that the contribution rate is not about efficiency. It is a sophisticated matrix that include people skills, measurable work, interhuman relations and even time spent in the community building. We use that indicator not to measure people's productivity in the narrow sense of efficiency but as a way to measure their flourishing."

Takahashi continued, "We must understand why people behave the way they do and find out how we can help everyone in society achieve their highest potential. We have to identify where their lack of drive stem from--is it because they are not able to find work that fulfils them? If so, is the issue with the education system or the support from the Guiders? It just means that there's work cut out in terms of strengthening certain aspects of the State. Let's look more deeply. Bring me reports on the satisfaction levels of the students in their placements, as well as the perception the citizens in that Dome feel towards work in society. Make sure it includes the individual indicators of success rates, wellbeing, interrelations, interactions, and ability to hold oneself together. We'll reconvene in two days."

Takahashi was in a meeting with his co-workers reviewing the data on the status of resources in the Pragmatic State and how the State was faring. As the Deputy Head of Resource Allocation, Strategic Planning, his role is to assess the current allocation of resources and propose areas in which resources can be channelled into for the betterment of society.

Food, energy, waste management in the Pragmatic State was sustainable and nearly all materials used were recyclable. Environmental emissions from human activities were also neutralised by the Terraformers, and population control was balanced against resources availability and required productivity projection. Having an overview of these conditions was the duty of Takahashi's department.

Bearing in mind the three mottos of society, Takahashi had to chart out his own interpretation of how achieving the three mottos would translate into actual policies related to resource allocation. The responsibility was tremendous. Together with his team, they had the power to propose and decide which aspects of the State gets emphasized and which, in turn, would take a step back. Each decision made had a real-world impact on everyone in society. He had always found the process of deciding what should or ough*t* to be done to be one of heavy responsibility.

At that level of policy planning, it was also easy to see people as numbers and figures, but Takahashi was keenly aware of that and constantly guarded himself against that—he was always reminding himself that he had to continue to stay connected to the ground. He had to be able to see every individual as dignified actor who made decisions based on specific logic and circumstances. It was precisely his cautiousness that has led him to rise through the ranks. He held himself to the highest standards, never letting himself get away with any mistakes. The Services was a meaningful place for Takahashi. When he put his analytical skills to work, he was alive. Yet at the same time, he often found himself asking if he was doing the right thing, making the best decisions. He knew he was holding a tremendous amount of responsibility. Everything he approved immediately affected the lives of people.

After the end of the meeting, he made his way out and headed for the Defence Department in Hindhidel district where the Defence Department was located.

****

Resource allocation in the Pragmatic state is centred around the three mottos of society and establishing pathways to achieve those goals. With an abundance of natural resources made possible through technological advancement, the food and energy are consumed in a sustainable manner. Waste is also disposed of responsibly—beyond just carbon footprint, all forms of pollution and emissions are controlled. Nearly all materials are recyclable. Industrial-scale environmental rehabilitation and correction is required to offset human footprint.

Policies of population control are well implemented and scientifically based on the availability of sustainable resources and productivity. Within the population planning teams, population targets are revised according to projections of resource availability. Part of the role of the Resource Allocation department is to monitor the impact of human activity on the environment and ensuring that usage is kept at regulatory defined levels set by the Resource Department according to the population level and progress of the society.

The environment on Earth is maintained at pre-industrialisation levels. Thus, there are massive green vegetations and abundance of animals. This is all achieved due to scientific advancements, human ingenuity, and collective society effort.

Where the Pragmatic State exists, the weather is temperate. With the capacity and technology of the Pragmatic State, previously inhospitable hot and cold regions of the planet were terraformed to support comfortable living. Without the baggage of familial relationships, people no longer have the concept and emotional attachment or conflicts arising from holding on to generations of ancestral homes, communities, specific plots of land. Assets are not defined by what one owned but by the actions one takes and the skills that one brings and contributes.

Since the State is the controller of most resources, social programmes abound. While the private sector drives most commercial activities, the State owns majority of economic assets. Sectors that are exclusively driven and funded by State include: basic to tertiary education, local transport, utilities, and healthcare.

****

The public sector was what Takahashi knew about all his life. Deep down, he was a staunch believer of the Pragmatic State. Besides working in the Resource Allocation Department, he was also heavily involved in Defence. He had demonstrated his competency and foresight in the managing and planning of resources and had recently been allocated work in the Defence Department to work on international relations through Defence planning. Arriving at the Defence Department, Takahashi was inspecting the new machinery in the warehouse and obtaining information on the latest space defence equipment and upgrades.

"And how are the StellarNets coming along?" he asked Norman, the reporting officer as they walked and viewed the production line.

"They are doing well, Mr. Takahashi," replied Norman, "We're currently adding a few more features, including long- and short-range proximity sensors to the StellarNets so that they'll be able to detect potential offense or suspicious activity that is coming through Space."

"Sounds like they are well underway then," Takahashi commented.

"If you don't mind me asking, I have been pondering about our Defence strategy and what function it serves in today's context. We live in relatively peaceful times. Even nations that have not converted to Pragmatism maintain a good relationship with us," Norman said.

"Well, you are right to say that we live in relatively peaceful times. The way I see it, Defence is partly about progress—developing the technology we have in space, while at the same time the fear of the unknown drives innovation," said Takahashi. "But I've only recently taken over this portfolio, and I am not sure if my understanding is complete either," Takahashi added, reminding himself that he does not have the full knowledge to be able to lead his team.

"What you said about progress resonated with me. Sometimes, I do think we need something to work towards. And defence is interesting because it is about understanding the known and the unknown threats, while at the same time, there is something innovative," Norman commented. "Ever since you joined the Defence Department, the direction has shifted a little."

Takahashi held his breath at what seemed like a verdict on his ability and performance hitherto.

"Edwin was a much more hawkish leader. He understood defence primarily as power... He was aggressive about pushing for the latest technology as a show of power. Ever since you took over three years ago, I see the emphasis on innovation and exploration. You gave us time to develop the technology."

Takahashi exhaled, mindful about being discreet with regard to how much other people's perceptions and self-doubt affected him.

"Thank you for your honest opinion, Norman. I appreciate it," Takahashi replied. "Well, I have to head to the other departments in Defence to check in on the colony shield system."

****

Military is hinged upon in defensive planning capabilities. While strategy is designed by people, the execution is done by systems and robots. This is spearheaded exclusively by the Pragmatic State—no private sector defence companies were allowed as it is an industry purely for society protection and not for-profit. Defence industries is off-limits for private sector to avoid instances where profits drive conflicts. Historically, profit driven private sector activities have frequently resulted in inequality, chaos, and conflicts on a massive scale just to enrich a small group of people.

Since the establishment of the Pragmatic State, there are lesser military conflicts between similar social systems. The focus is on society improvement and mankind's progress. Any major conflict, especially drastic actions of invasion of any kind, will require a vast majority approval from citizens which is difficult to obtain. Due to the nature of the Pragmatic State, migration and integration across similar social systems are allowed under population control guidelines, but not with external backward societies.

****

***

It was Takahashi's weekly coffee time with his best friend, Eva.

"How has it been in the Defence Department? I hear that there are some exciting developments," Eva asked, jet black eyes looking in anticipation as she sipped on her coffee.

"You know me. I can never quite feel like I am fully integrated in any one job. Even in Resource Allocation, which is supposedly my domain for more than 20 years, I don't always feel that I am fully competent to lead all these people under me. There is an awful amount of responsibility and power that I hold," Takahashi said solemnly, deep in thought.

"We'll never have all the right answers Takahashi. It is a constant battle that we have. Every system will have its flaws," Eva asserted, tucking her black hair behind her ears, ready for a debate.

Takahashi returned a look of disagreement—he fully believed in the system and would not take opposition well. Eva was Takahashi's long-time friend and a judge in the Superior Court. Takahashi and Eva have a longstanding disagreement about the flaws of the system. Takahashi was an ardent believer of the Pragmatic State. He believes that the laws and rules helped to keep things in equilibrium. For him, society is held together by these rules that create a balance. The three mottos of society were his mantra. He bought into them wholeheartedly–they were fundamental to his belief system.

"Take for example the system of policing. It seems overly rigid to me sometimes. The citizen implant that every individual has contains recordings that become accessible. In a way, that makes my life as a judge straight-forward because I can immediately see if a crime has been committed. While some people criticise it as hyper-surveillance, I understand where the State's intention in deterring crime and eliminating mistakes in meting out punishment. What I disagree with, is the way the severity of punishment is decided upon" Eva said. "As judges, we get a list of guidelines for judgement that correspond with the crimes committed, but at the moment there is no space rulings that allows the judge to exercise empathy."

"I think the spirit of that practice is to eliminate the possibility for a margin of error that might be caused by perceptions or emotions. Isn't it good that there is clarity?" Takahashi rebutted.

"Tak, I know what you mean. The moment there is room for the judge to play bigger role, there is a possibility of overly heavy or light sentences. But know that these rules are what they are because people set them too," Eva said.

Takahashi stopped sipping his coffee and looked up. Eva continued, "Humans are always changing. The laws and systems, too, must continually evolve. Besides, the law is never fool proof. It works on a logical and rational system, but we all know that humans behave irrationally. That is why, despite knowing that undeniable evidence will be recorded through the implants, people still continue to commit crimes. The irrationality of human behaviour cannot be predicted by a logical system, which is why I do believe that systems have to continually evolve."

"There's no end to this discussion. You know that we disagree on our faith in the system. But I am starting to see what you mean by the need for people to continually update the system. It needs to be a live system that can accommodate change," said Takahashi. "We talk about our disagreements all the time and I am appreciative of the honesty that you always bring Eva. Your perspectives always counter mine in ways that helps me see with a little more breadth."

"Having this space also helps me to process my thoughts, Tak, "said Eva.

"I'm going to need a lot of this in the next couple of months to come since I have been nominated to run for elections as the High Rep for Resource Allocation Services. Being Deputy Head in the Resource Allocation Services and the Defence Department, I will now need to drop my Defence portfolio if I get elected. The thing is, I don't know if I'm ready to take over the helm and be placed in such an important position," said Takahashi.

"Well, we will definitely keep this going for as long as we are friends!" Eva assured Tak. "For now, I should probably get back to finish up some work."

"I'll let you get on with it then," Tak said.

"Catch you soon!" Eva replied before hurrying off.

***

Adjusting her collar in front of the mirror, Eva traced her silhouette as she prepares herself to enter the courtroom. Being precise and immaculate was part of the job—both inside and out. She demanded that of herself every day. In the courtroom, every decision carried weight. Responsibility hung on her shoulders. While the facts laid bare and the guidelines were in place to guide the process, there was a certain weight, perhaps an emotional attachment, that came with being the one responsible for delivering the sentence.

Authoritative and stoic as she was in the courtroom, she sometimes felt a sense of helplessness. She held so much power and yet there was no room for a softer sentence once culpability was confirmed. The role of the judge was to assess the information and ascertain the circumstances in which someone committed a crime. Guidelines helped to determine the sentence the culprit would receive.

As she took her seat in the court room, the bailiff spoke, "All rise. Department One of the Superior Court is now in session. Judge Eva presiding. Please take your seat."

"Good morning, ladies and gentlemen. Calling the case of the People of the State versus Connor," Eva said with resolutely. "Are both sides ready?"

"Ready for the People, Your Honour."

"Ready for the Defence, Your Honour."

"Your Honour, the defendant has been charged with the crime of murder of 38-year-old female, Felica. A review of the evidence will show that he murdered the deceased along the sidewalk of the Hamilton district at 8 pm on 30 November last year. The evidence I present will prove to you that the defendant is guilty as charged and deserves capital punishment."

"Your Honour, while the evidence provides undeniable evidence of my client's culpability, there is sufficient circumstantial reasons to warrant a lighter sentence for my client. This was a woman who had inflicted tremendous psychological trauma and pain on my client. His act was committed after suffering from years of psychological trauma caused by the deceased. Therefore, my client would like to seek a lighter sentence than what would have been dispensed for murder."

A crime of passion, Eva thought to herself. That always made coming to a decision more tumultuous. Crimes of passion involved delving into the murky waters of emotions and psyche. The job of untangling the threads of blame and culpability was never clear-cut. While the visible act of crime was undeniably wrong, the invisible crimes exacted had to be so thoroughly traumatic to lead someone to the moment of the macabre.

"The prosecution may call on the first piece of evidence," Eva commanded.

"The People call on the implant data of the accused, Your Honour," said the prosecutor.

The footage from the accused's implant played on the screen. In the footage, he crept up to the deceased and stabbed her gruesomely in the stomach. Blood oozed out from the wound as she fell to the ground feebly, clutching the knife that was now firmly planted in her torso. He stared at the withering and writhing body, stumbled a few steps backward. Kneeling on the ground he began to sob uncontrollably. The pain and agony of his cries struck Eva. It was a complex of emotions. *What did the deceased do to bring out the violence of someone so capable of expressing and recognising the extremity of the act?* she wondered. It was this complex of human emotions that Eva felt the prevailing system of justice was not advanced enough to account for.

It was the Defence's turn to make their case and prove the motivation of Connor in his murder attempt. The position of the Defence was never about facts—that was always covered by the State's all-encompassing surveillance and data. The culpability of the act was never debated. What had room for debate was the motivations that led someone, who, in full knowledge that their implants would be dredged up as incriminating evidence, would follow through with the crime. Through the cross-questioning, it came to light that he was under much distress throughout his relationship with the deceased. It was a toxic relationship where there had been physical and verbal abuse throughout their ten years of marriage.

After the prosecutor was done cross examining Connor, Eva spoke, "Does the Defence have any questions?"

"Yes, your Honour," the Defence lawyer spoke.

"Describe your relationship with the deceased," the Defence lawyer asked.

"She was my wife," Connor replied.

"How was your relationship with her like?"

"It was tenuous," Connor said as he got emotional, "because the relationship was toxic. I was under a lot of mental stress when I was with her. It has been ten years of physical and verbal abuse. Not only did she cheat on me, but she was also constantly putting me down, hurling degrading words at me. Every single day for the last ten years of my life, I have been living in fear. Every mistake I made; I was punished for it. I lost my dignity and my ability to stand up for myself."

"Why did you attack your wife on that fateful day?"

"It was a usual morning—with the paternalistic and degrading scolding. Her last words before she left the house was: "You're worse than a dog! No different from an animal. Can you imagine my disgust waking up next to you every day?" My spirits hit rock-bottom, and I was destroyed. My wife had just left the house for work, leaving me in shambles. The final straw came when she summoned me to where she was at her hoverboard with a whistle, "Come over you fucking dog! Fetch me my visor. The sun is scorching, and I need to be shaded on my commute to work," Connor began sobbing uncontrollably.

"I lost it. I was no longer human in her eyes. She treated me worse than an animal!" his voice trembling and trailing off as he spoke. He was internally destroyed. Shaking uncontrollably and utterly distraught, he buried his face in his hands, incapacitated.

There was a lump in Eva's throat. Connor shared vulnerably and she bought his story, but she was cognisant that his testament would not hold up in court. Unless there was a way to justify acts of violence that stemmed from psychological trauma, he was going to receive capital punishment for his deeds. At that thought, she felt her cheeks flushing and her body burning up. These were the cases that slipped through the cracks. The was no sympathy for Connor.

The rest of the court proceedings went on according to plan perfectly, mechanically, as it always did. Eva was part of that engine and machine. It was difficult keeping the balance of impartiality as a judge and empathy as a human being. Extricating herself from the emotional investment, she activated her device to call out a hologram. On her screen, she could see the individual notes that the jury and panel comprising psychologists and counsellors were adding into the system. Most of them were not convinced by Connor—they had voted for capital punishment.

The law was rigid that way. The guilty would either be deemed as hopelessly incorrigible, thereby receiving capital punishment, or sentenced to re-education. There was no in-between. She could feel her dissatisfaction mounting. Petty crimes would mean receiving re-education as the punishment but anything beyond that meant capital punishment. *How strict and unreasonable can the law get?* Eva asked. Court proceedings unfolded regimentally. More needs to go into the understanding of why such crimes happen—was there something to be done in education and in understanding the motivations of these human behaviours?

Hold yourself in the space of being a judge, Eva. Slap on that poker face, keep your distance, stay detached, she chanted to herself. For her to continue with the proceedings and fulfil her duty in the courtroom she would need to extract her personal emotions from the situation.

She concluded the court proceeding eventually by sentencing Connor to capital punishment with a nearly unanimous vote on Connor's fate. She announces with a cold detachment, "Court is adjourned." She wished for a way that the law could exercise empathy, to change and adapt with the times.

****

In the Pragmatic State, all rules and regulations are approached scientifically. New laws and amendments are proposed by judges and subject matter experts, reviewed by High Order, and voted by all citizens. Science and technology has enabled all citizens to participate through direct democracy and direct exercising of their rights. There is a clear distinction between the Judicial branch in the implementation and execution of the law, while the Executive branch lead by the High Order oversees formulating strategy for the State and the subsequent execution to plan.

Defendants in courts do not make their case on grounds of whether the deed is done but on the motivation for the crime. The high level of surveillance and monitoring mean that no crime goes undocumented. Within the stringent system, there is no wriggle room on legalities, technicalities, and loopholes. Sentencing by judges are regularly collected and analysed to check for outliers. Technology is also harnessed extensively in the analysis of data—AI, machine learning and sophisticated data analysis technology is used to aggregate and analyse data. Since Pragmatism is the central principle governing the State, sentencing is done swiftly, with little delay and wastage of the State's resources.

Generally, a high level of monitoring and education results in high compliance of law. Citizens are tagged with real time locational data and audio-visual recording which are uploaded to the Core system. The high monitoring and data collection made police investigation, sentencing precise and prompt. Mainstream illegal activities are also nearly non-existent. The physical act of law enforcement is done by robots.

In the Pragmatic State, a person that is found guilty would either receive re-education, deterrence through short-term incarceration, or capital punishment for incorrigible offenders deemed incapable of being integrated back into society. The considerations rest upon individual circumstances and the psychological states at the time. Long-term incarceration is not an option as it is considered a waste of resources—the State should not be wasting resources on facilities that will separate offenders from society forever. The harshness of the law reflected the pragmatic nature of the State.

Among the many crimes, corruption and discrimination were considered the gravest of crimes because of the potential factionalism. The State was extremely stringent about deeds that result in factionalism. There was zero tolerance for discrimination in the form of unjust or prejudicial treatment that is given to an individual based his or her habits, skin colour and background. No harm should be done to another human being because of their way of life.

****

***

"How are you feeling?" Eva asked Takahashi, "it's the start of the elections this week."

“Feeling apprehensive, I suppose. If this really comes true, I’ll really be in office. It’s that responsibility that I fear,” Takahashi replied, “I'm not sure if I am really as capable as what people make me to be."

Takahashi and Eva were taking a stroll and walking after having lunch at their usual hangout at the café near Garmond District.

"It has been such a busy week putting together all the materials to be made available to the public and preparing myself for the discussion,” said Takahashi. "I had to consider who to approach for my peer reviews and make preparations so that the Election Office is able to reach out to them. Since the review is kept a secret, I had no idea what they had said about me until it was released this morning! They really flattered me,” Takahashi exclaimed.

"Tak, you are too modest. Anyone reading your CV would immediately know that you are a man of high calibre. Have some confidence and faith in yourself, my friend!” said Eva. "Your response to the question given to all the candidates were brilliant. It was about your vision for the future of the Pragmatic State and how you think we can progress as a society. I loved that you took a rather human view from your position in the Resource Allocation Department. You answered beautifully and honestly about the prevailing challenge of needing to look at the aspirations, hope and desires of citizens to understand motivations behind every individual. It really humanised the Services,” Eva said. "I have always found that to be your strength Tak—the fact that you would always try to bring in empathetic perspectives into the way you allocate and run resources."

"I'm really just doing what I think anyone in my position ought to be doing. To be honest, I find it absolutely surreal that I'm running in the elections. Never have I thought I would be where I'm at today. The lingering doubt about my ability to pull this off never dissipates. I battle with the need to check my own intentions and capability constantly... at times, it does become crippling,” confessed Takahashi. Continuing with a sigh, Takahashi said “I’ve always only been on the side evaluating the performance of candidates, reviewing their profile and achievements before I make the decision to vote for anyone. Having gone through the process, my sensitivity has heightened. It makes me excited but also worried about how I can live up to people's expectations if I'm elected to the High Order."

"Oh Tak, you worry wart! I believe you have given it your all. Besides, all candidate's achievements and credentials throughout their lives have been made available online for all to see, judge and decide. And that is the whole point of having candidates judged solely on their competency and not on oratory prowess and powers of persuasion if it is not backed by true substance. Shouldn't you be aware of the intent of such a system designed by the State that you so adore and support?"

What Eva said made sense, Takahashi thought. If he believed in the system, he ought to believe that the truly capable candidate for the High Rep will be found through the system. The system would have accounted for all possibilities.

With the calm that mirrored the park they had arrived at, he said, "Thank you, Eva. This confidence you have in me means so much to me." They sat down on the bench in the park, continuing their conversation about systems, politics and governance. They rattled and prattled on about everything and anything under the sun. Takahashi always appreciated the camaraderie that he shared with Eva.

Before parting ways, Eva turned to Takahashi and said with the sincerest grin, "I know you will win this, Tak. You're competent through-and-through and you do everything with the purest intentions. I can't imagine anyone better than you in this position."

****

> Elections in the Pragmatic State is usually held over a week. Candidates are nominated by their colleagues in the Services based on their track record and competencies. Once selected, their CVs will be released during election week along with interviews with the candidates and the candidate's peers. The focus is in equal parts on the candidate's past achievements as well as how they have rectified errors of their own projects and judgements. All historical records of

the individual will be released during elections, and citizens can access the CVs of all candidates via their interface.

In particular, all candidates will also be asked to respond to the same set of questions to showcase their perspectives while offering them an opportunity to present their visions for the society through their answers. These video responses are recorded and made available to the public during the elections. In this segment, they are typically asked on their previous policies and what they aim to do if they are elected.

In the Pragmatic State, elections are designed to be an activity that focused on the track record and achievements of the candidates instead of what they are able to promise, or their ability to rally crowds. Since people in the Services and High Order seldom appear in the media, citizens have to judge the suitability of the candidates based on their ideas on governance but that will always be backed by their credentials. For all serving in the Services, they have been taught throughout their careers that these are positions to serve all citizens and the State, and not for themselves. Therefore, they avert the media attention on an individual level but instead choosing to live a life away from limelight to focus on the work and results that they deliver.

****

It was 7 am in the morning and Takahashi was getting ready for his first day as the High Rep of Resource and Allocation. True to Eva's prediction, Takahashi won the elections despite strong competition. While everyone was celebrating his victory, a part of him worried about his ability to perform up to task. Everyone seemed to put him on the pedestal, which only increased his internal pressure. The sight of people's disappointed countenance was his deepest fear. Being responsible for the lives of others was a weight he eschewed carrying for fear of failing to meet the expectations of others. The first order of things would be to nominate and select the leader of the High Rep, the Chairperson, from among the 11 High Reps. The Chairperson was more of a figurehead and facilitator without veto power—the High Order was designed to have a flat hierarchy.

With trepidation, Takahashi buttoned up his sleeves and looked at himself in the mirror while he got ready for his first day in office as a High Rep. His head was spinning with excitement and doubt at this newfound responsibility. His worries and fears were amplified tenfold. *How will he ensure that he was always doing a good job and always sure of what people on the ground needed?* he thought. He wanted to continue to serve the people the best but there was a nagging fear he had about whether he really deserved to be voted into power.

He made his way to the Tower where the High Order's main office was located. The building was basking in the full glory of the golden sunlight. Upon arrival, he was welcomed by a delegate who was assigned the task of orientating him on his first day in the High Order.

"My name is Thomson and I will be orientating you on your first day. How are you doing today, Sir?" said Thomson.

"Good so far. It has been a surreal week and morning," Takahashi replied.

"Congratulations once again for being elected to the High Order. The agenda for today is for me to bring you to the different places in this building—your office and conference rooms—and for you to meet the rest of the High Reps. Shall we begin?" Thomson gestured towards the lift to another floor.

Takahashi was shown the facilities in the building that he could access, as well as the people who would be supporting him in his work as the High Rep for Resource Allocation. Done with the orientation, Thomson brought Takahashi to the meeting room where he would meet the other High Reps for the first time.

"This is the end of your orientation and I'll leave you to attend your meeting. If you have any further questions after today, please feel free to contact your assigned advisor whose details are already on ECHO."

"Thank you, Thomson for the orientation. I appreciate it," said Takahashi.

There was a gush of fresh air when the door opened. Five other High Reps have already arrived and were talking to one another.

"It's nice to finally meet you, Takahashi," Paul, who was elected High Rep of Public Health spoke. "I have heard much about you and the good work that you've been doing in the Resource Allocation Department and was looking forward to finally meeting you in person."

"And I could say the same to you too, Paul. I truly admire the dedication that you show in your work," Takahashi replied.

"Hi gentlemen," Darren interrupted, "I'd like to introduce myself. I am Darren from Arts and Culture, and I am honoured to be here among some of the most brilliant minds in the State."

"Such a pleasure to meet you, Darren. I have read up about the push you have been making towards getting more people to dialogue and discuss about pertinent concerns and picking apart the existing issues that can be address in our system," Paul replied. "I am a huge patron of the arts, and I am currently also sitting on the board of several arts non-profit organisations, thinking about how they can harness technology more in cultural production."

Aware of the dangers of collusion because of the overlaps in interest, Takahashi quickly steered the topic towards the experience everyone had with regard to elections. Everyone was wary of the grave offense of colluding in the Services. While it was acceptable to talk about personal lives at work, any such activities that benefited a small collective was not allowed. People in the Services, especially, need to be careful not to form cliques that might serve self-interests—all actions should serve the State as a whole instead of individuals. Since joining the Services, people have been taught not to form coalitions with each other at work. If found to be forming cliques that benefited personal businesses or organisations, the State would take legal actions with severe punishments against the people in question. Within this context, people kept their boundaries clear.

When everyone arrived, a hologram appeared to congratulate and welcome all the High Reps of the Services. Accordingly, all 11 of them were asked to do a formal introduction of themselves to the other Reps. Takahashi was nervous. He still had lingering doubts about his worthiness and ability to lead people from this position. Shortly after the introductions, the hologram prompted the High Reps to appoint the figurehead of the High Rep. "In the High Order, decisions are made by everyone in the High Rep–all had equal power. The primary role of the Chairperson is to facilitate meetings and steer the direction of the conversations," the hologram clarified. Through each of their interfaces, they reviewed the CV of every High Rep and cast a vote for the Chairperson in secrecy.

Alvin from Defence was eventually appointed as the Chairperson, and he would be the one responsible for leading discussions down the road. They spent the rest of the meetings getting to know the scope and visions each of them had for the departments they were heading. In the High Order, their main work was in collaboration and coordination between the Services–identifying where the synergies were. Takahashi was particularly intrigued because it was an opportunity to look at resource allocation vis-a-vis other departments, to understand how Resource Allocation's work fit with the rest of the Services. "We will need to reconvene in person in a month's time for a meeting with the previous High Order. But let's convene for weekly meetings to ensure that we put in place a certain cadence of work," Alvin said as he read the message that he had received on ECHO about the next meeting.

Takahashi thought it was strange that they did not get to meet the previous High Reps. That would have really eased him into work on the first day. As the meeting came to a close and people dispersed, Takahashi dialled the number for the advisor hoping to get some clarity on the next steps of being in office. They spent thirty minutes on the phone checking in and talking about the next steps ahead. It was a quick check-in, but Takahashi felt like he instantly connected with the advisor, Teegan, and the things he was telling Takahashi on the first day of work. He seemed to be able to read his mind and his anxieties about being in the High Order. He made a mental note to eventually meet Teegan for coffee.

Throughout the first month after taking over the High Order, Teegan was Takahashi's go-to person for advice on what to do and how he can manage his own anxieties in relation to the tasks at hand.

***

A month after their appointment, the High Order reconvened. They were each given time to meet with the previous High Reps. At some point, Daniel, the previous Chairperson and High Rep of Science & Technology gathered everyone.

"Gentlemen, thank you for taking time today to gather. The main purpose of today's session between the past and present High Order was to create an opportunity for you to connect and ask questions you may have after a month of working as a High Rep. At the same time, there is a special responsibility that the High Order of the State holds," Daniel spoke. "Recall all the times in your life that you may have met someone fleeting, whose presence in your life has helped you along in your journey–however big or small the impact. Since Reformation, the Founding Fathers have built an AI, in the form of a virtual persona, that aided individuals in society to work towards their purpose. This persona created by the AI existed as different characters and were projected directly into your mind via the Citizen Implant. This AI exists in assisting individuals to achieve their highest potential and fulfilling the three mottos."

Upon hearing the news, there was a moment of realisation–gasps and murmurings as the High Reps recalled the times they were helped by a conversation with or comment by a stranger. Takahashi realised that at different junctures of his life, he met people who were able to help him recalibrate and find his footing. Most of these encounters happened organically but they never last–it could be someone he struck a conversation with in the street or an acquaintance whom he would stop talking to after he had resolved his issues.

At that moment, individual holograms were projected in front of every member of the High Order. They saw the specific scenes and moments of their interactions with AI personas flashed before them. In front of Takahashi, he saw the old man whom he spoke to right after graduating from university. It was outside of campus on the last day of school. After that day, Takahashi was roped into the Services to help in the management of resources in the State. Takahashi saw himself lumbering across the street, head hung low. Although he did exceedingly well, as he always did, fear crippled him. *It began then*, he thought. *Being plagued and haunted by fear, expectations and self-doubt.*

That was the day he met that old man at the restaurant. Arriving at the doorstep of a Japanese restaurant, he made his way to the ramen booths, with the hope of having his meal on his own at the obscure corner of the empty restaurant. Shortly after he took his seat, an old man limped his way to the booth seat right next to his. Thereafter, they had a long chat about life, purpose and about his inner demons.

"Responsibility... is a scary thing. Within it lies the power for change, for good or for worse. Dwelling in your inefficacy dooms you, but wielding it bravely gives you a shot to bring about change," said the old man in the hologram.

Takahashi remembered how deeply those words impacted him. Those indelible words uplifted him and boosted him with a little more courage to take on the work in the Services. He never forgot it. It was those words of encouragement that led him to where he was. The hologram continued to playback the different moments the AI was activated to reach out to him.

The last person was the advisor whom he spoke to in the first month of being elected, who had helped him settle into the role. Everyone had their own "advisors" all throughout their lives to help them cope with their roadblocks towards realising their fullest potential. Shocking as it was, Takahashi was immensely grateful for such a system.

After every member completed their playback, Daniel spoke, "The AI system is the legacy of the Founding Fathers. It is imperative that the High Order continues to monitor the AI. The High Order has the veto power to change the system, amend it or even shut it down for good. It is entirely in the hands of the new High Order. During our tenure, we have made some modifications to the algorithm. You have to understand that it is not a perfect system. Things have to change and evolve based on needs of the time—that is reflective of spirit of the Pragmatic society. Regardless of the situation, Pragmatism as a way of living and approaching decision-making will never change. The same thing applies to the AI. If at any point in time the High Order decides that the society no longer requires the AI, then they are able to scrap it without holding back. Now, we leave it in your good judgement." With that, Daniel concluded the meeting.

***

It was the day of the Space Exploration Referendum. Eva got up early. The High Order had called for the referendum as and when they needed the citizen's direct opinions on the best course of action. With the technology in place, the High Order was able to disseminate information very swiftly and uniformly to the public. As such, people are able to enact change through their direct opinion instead of having a representative execute their wishes. As a mechanism, it was a way to put decision in the hands of the population. This only happened when it was considered a major decision by the High Order or as stipulated in the Constitution.

In this case, citizens were being consulted on the deployment of an ideal place they wanted to develop as an outpost but had recently discovered lifeform on the planet. Specifically, the referendum was about the series of guidelines and questions that would guide the expedition team on the new planets and the next course of action, as well as whether the work could continue. The first option comprised a series of questions that looked at the value of the planet with regard to the development of the human race. The second option was focused more on the principles and ethics of exploration– how much potential was there for lifeform to develop and whether the expansion on the territory would amount to denying life. The final option was about determining the possibility of a middle ground that could allow life to continue while still providing for some needs of the State.

Eva watched the panel discussions where tech experts talked and discussed the ethical principles of continuing and following through with developing the planet. The expert in question was a prolific writer and advisor when it came to policy making. He explained that the implications were profound if they did go ahead with the operations. The issue was about power and the exercising of one's right to rule over others. All throughout history, there were issues with the abuse of power, which was why there were several levels of checks and balances in the Services and even within the private sectors. If citizens decide to colonise the planet, they would be recognising the possibility that they might be destroying potential life forms that could have the possibility of evolution and growth. The expert pointed out that deciding to go ahead with operations meant that it was morally acceptable for someone more powerful to control and dominate another weaker person.

However, at the panel discussion, a science expert provided a counterpoint. He talked about the potential gains for humankind if the planet was further developed. Further, operations had already begun on the planet and investments had been made to develop an outpost. There could be potential losses and delay in timelines if the operations were withdrawn. He added that what was known were but guesses and possibilities rather than proven facts that these nascent lifeforms, which were not detected when the explorers first landed on the planet, would continue to grow and evolve into intelligent life forms. At the rapid rate in which research was taking place, there would come a point in which scientists and researchers would be able to study the species in-depth, understand the lifeform's possibility of evolution and provide the conditions for that to happen. He was of the view that we ought to move ahead with the planned operations while monitoring the development of these lifeforms. Provisions could also be made for co-existence and scientific research could yield new technologies that might allow the lifeforms to continue to grow.

The economist concurred on the same point, saying the losses would be significant because of the sunk cost of developing the outpost. Citizens would be pulling out based on a mere possibility that the lifeform would not be able to exist alongside human developments. Giving up the planet now would also mean more resources would be needed to search for alternative planets as exploration outposts.

Eva was invigorated by the discussions and conversations. She felt that more of such conversations and panel discussions ought to happen more often–it brought critical perspectives that members of the public ought to consider. She thought it was a brilliant way to educate the public on a particular topic, subject or issue.

Done with the panel discussion, Eva read through all the resources that were made available online for all citizens for the entire duration of the referendum. Scouring through the files and perusing them with the utmost detail that a judge can bring, Eva began to see and understand the full picture of the issue at hand.

At the end of the day, Eva still stood her ground and voted against the continued operations on that planet. She was someone concerned with the ethical implications of all the policies in the State and what valuation each of those policies represented. She wished for more opportunities that could mobilise every single citizen in exercising their rights after doing their due diligence to understand the varying perspectives.

This was how the society could move itself forward–constant dialogue and conversations on the issues that people faced in society. Having the platform to be able to exercise their own power and decision-making rights to directly affect the outcomes of issues would be important. For all that Eva felt was lacking in the current justice system, she recognised that there were aspects of the system that revealed the right intentions of the Founding Fathers who wanted to create a system that would enable people to directly appoint people in the Services—to inch towards what would be a true democracy. No system is perfect. Eva recognised that. However, a system that continuously allows for change and adaptation might be what 'perfect' means. 'Perfection' laid in the humility to recognise that humans would always be a work in progress and that the only way people could guard against their darkness was to recognise that they were fallible, though they should never stop trying.

****

The Referendum can be called either by the High Order or triggered by citizens in times of perceived crisis. Citizens can call for a Vote of No Confidence to remove the Chairperson, any specific High Rep or the entire High Order. This is a check-and-balance mechanism which is deeply respected and executed by all branches of the Judicial and Military, to prevent abuse of power by the governing High Order.

****

Epilogue

"I'll miss the sea, but a person needs new experiences. They jar something deep inside, allowing him to grow. Without change something sleeps inside us, and seldom awakens." – Frank Herbert, Dune

The world was ablaze, smothering in its own disease. Frederick stood gravely in the tower from which he governed the city. A workers' protest was ongoing at the docks to the Northeast of the Tower, while a demonstration was raging along the streets south of the Tower. The police and the military had been mobilised to quell the unrest. *A band-aid solution*, Frederick told himself.

He looked at the city with a strange comingling of love and hate. *Was this how God saw the city of Sodom? Torn between a love that sought salvation for humanity, and an inexplicable abhorrence towards the rancour of human behaviour?* Deep down, Frederick knew that it would take something fundamental and drastic to completely change the course of humanity. People have been going at it for thousands of years and nothing has worked out. Inequality has persisted; class divisions remain entrenched; power continued to be abused. The society was at its breaking point. In the past 20 years of his career, Frederick had been working at building his political base in preparation for the moment that he might need to make this decision. While planning for it, he had always held out for the sliver of hope that things would never need to come to this point. He spent years filling the ranks with his trusted advisors, playing the game of politics so that one day he could use the power that he had accumulated to initiate change for a system that was rotten to the core.

He called for the emergency meeting ever since the series of violent civil rights protests began. The seams that so precariously held the society together–the false sense of harmony–was tearing apart. He was going to announce and decree the execution of the Reformation–the plan to fundamentally change the rules and logic that governed society.

"Things are not looking great, Frederick," Johnson muttered as he opened the room of the conference room Frederick was in.
"I'm fully aware, John," he responded solemnly. "The time might have come for us to execute the plan that we've hatched all these years."

John's eyes widened with surprise upon hearing the news, but they quickly resolved into a knowing look of resignation. The advisors of the government understood that this day might come. Following the lead of Frederick, they devised a new world order to address the perennial problems that humanity was never able to rid itself of. When everyone arrived, Frederick announced, "Gentlemen, over the past couple of weeks, we have watched our world implode. The seed of every single problem that unravelled in the past month was sown even before we were born. What we are seeing now should come as no surprise to anyone."

"Everyone in this room was fully cognisant of the interconnectedness and the systemic nature of the problems in our society." Frederick paused, took a quick breath, and emphatically concluded, "We have arrived at our breaking point." A moment of silence followed, as if everyone held their breaths momentarily.

"Today, our purpose is to flesh out the details of the Pragmatic State which we have been talking about. It is time to jolt the people and wake them up from their slumber," Frederick remarked.

"Are you sure we have to resort to that, Frederick," Arthur inquired. The room began to be filled with chatter.

"The world is burning. And it is time to remake it," said Frederick. There was silence in the room. An air of agreement at the state of things.

In the hours that ensued, the advisors relooked at the plans that they had been preparing conceptually but are now finally concretising. It was a war room of debates, arguments, ideas, and agreement. In the different discussion groups, the advisors presented their perspectives.

"As we distilled the perennial issue of inequality and hoarding of resources, we have decided that the root issue is one of legacy resources and assets. The rich continue to accumulate wealth because of family histories. What if there is a system where wealth and power are not compounded across generations but instead returned to the State to be circulated and redistributed?" Arthur presented. "However, to do that requires the radical and drastic measure of disallowing people from having relationships with descendants. Perhaps that is the only way people will begin to realise that there is no point in hoarding resources – when they know they have no one to pass it on to. After all, man comes into the world with nothing and will leave in the same state, so why should there be legacy hoarding?" Arthur remarked.

Adding on to that train of thought, Simon added, "The other root issue of wealth disparity is the lack of a truly meritocratic system. Since there will not be any families in the way we know it now, everyone will be brought up by the State, without having the head start accrued through wealth, power, and family networks. Everyone will grow up being exposed to the same, centralised education system and given an equal opportunity to develop their interests."

It was a dangerous and yet seductive plan. One that was difficult to swallow but undeniably valid in its logic. "I may not fully agree with it at an emotional level. But in principle, I concur with what you are proposing," said Frederick. Coming up with a system and concretising it was not easy. Yet everyone knew that it was what they had to do if they wanted to see the world change for the better. Bringing together the best minds in the nation, the advisors eventually agreed on the three core mottos of the New World Order.

All of society was gathered around the principles embodied by the three mottos:

- For progress of all Mankind
- For benefit of the State
- For living a meaningful life

While it was a thorny issue, the advisors agreed that some measure of population control needed to happen. As it was, the earth was being exploited and ill-treated by humans. That cannot continue if the human race wanted to survive as a species. In principle, there needed to be responsible and sustainable use of resources on Earth via population control and a mixture of private sector driven and State planned economy. "The State must take control of the key industries that will help to maintain the balance of the social fabric," Marcus, the Minister of Public Health asserted. "The tech, business, production and innovation space should be dominated by private sector, although private ownership rules should be revised accordingly."

"Fundamentally, people need to shift their mindsets from an individualism to a utilitarian view that prioritises collective interests and collective good. People need to stop thinking in terms of 'I' and move towards 'we'. All the principles we have devised are geared towards achieving this mindset in society," said Frederick.

"I agree with you wholeheartedly Frederick." Ronald from Ministry of Public Affairs stated. "The society is too divisive. Politics are splitting people's allegiance, polarising society. I believe that differences are inevitable, but that people need to have the maturity to accept, embrace and learn from differences. In fact, differences should be celebrated, but right now the democratic system is broken. Politicians are leveraging on differences to lobby for support–all for the sake of winning more voters and supporters for the self-serving aim to keep themselves in power. A political career has over the years degenerated to somewhat like a reality popularity show of deceit and self-interests without the true aim of public service," Ronald continued. "We need to abolish political lobbying, collusion, and populism. Only the truly capable should be responsible for governing the country and ultimately leading the people."

They all came to an agreement, however, that they were fallible people coming up with a system that was not tested. They agreed that systems need to be in place so that certain structures can guide organisation, however, the system must continuously evolve. No system should remain forever unchanging. What the advisors agreed was a proposal that had to be tested and continuously refined according to the times. Circumstances could change but being pragmatic and continuously evolving should be at the core of the New World Order.

It was an exacting system that the advisors came up with. Everyone was spent—drained by the process of internal debate and negotiation but also exhausted from the monumental task of redesigning life. "We've created a harsh and exacting system," Desmond spoke with resignation. "And yet, it does seem like the lesser evil for now. I hope that future generations will fine-tune what we have put in place to make it a better reality."

"Perhaps the only way to deal with the decay in society is to introduce something so radical that it can fundamentally change the way we live," Tarun commented. He was right. When something has decayed beyond redemption, it was best to tear it down and rebuild from scratch.

"But how will men continue to stay on the path of progress? Technology and Science," said Wilson. "There must be something, an engine that can keep people going, searching, working and progressing. Aren't we all also on a constant search as well? We all need that."

"If there's anything that we've learnt from the past, it is that humans can't help themselves, not completely. What if we harnessed the technology of AI to guide humans, keep them on track as much as possible?" Arthur suggested.

"I'm not sure about AI..." Tarun retorted, "there could be complications. I'm not confident in using an algorithm to override human decisions."

"I'm not saying that AI is better or that it would supersede humans. I, for one, do not ever wish that for the human race. My point, rather is that there is a potential benefit to be reaped from utilising AI—to analyse human behaviour and nudge us to the right society goals. Humans would still have the ultimate say," Arthur continued.

"If we are able to work the logic of our system and New World Order into an AI system, perhaps it could help us bring the plan to fruition, and even make it better," Frederick commented. "There is potential in this. If there are 'guardian angels' programmed with the core principles of the new society we are creating, they could perhaps show up in people's lives to lead and guide them in accordance to the values that should be upheld in society."

"I think that ultimately, humans will need to hold the key to this," said Ronald. "We can have a select few in the leadership position, who are aware of the existence of the AI and they will have to undertake the role of monitoring the AI system. They will then have the power to make an executive decision to terminate the AI system, temporarily halt, or upgrade the system. The role of the AI, is to appear in the lives of individuals as and when it is needed, to encourage and spur people on based on their potential."

"We don't need to come up with the perfect system," said Frederick. "The whole spirit of Pragmatism is that regardless of the times and the change in circumstances, the approach will always be pragmatic in taking the course of action that would yield progress and the highest good. It's about taking incremental steps towards a better humankind, to continuously search for a better way of working and being," Frederick concluded. "I believe we have a skeletal structure of what could be a possible future. It's a drastic change and I hope it can reform the society."

This was how the Reformation, which eventually created the Pragmatic State, came about.

THE END

In support of the author's effort to conduct extensive research, promote Pragmatism thinking, and widescale implementation to solve current societal problems, it will be greatly appreciated if you can donate and support our cause at www.pragmatismfuture.com . All contributions regardless of the amount will be greatly appreciated. We also call on supporters of Pragmatism to reach out and share with us your thoughts on how we can work together today, to make tomorrow a better place for everyone.

www.ingramcontent.com/pod-product-compliance
Ingram Content Group UK Ltd.
Pitfield, Milton Keynes, MK11 3LW, UK
UKHW041843200726
13854UKWH00005BA/2034